FANCY GOODS

OPEN ALL NIGHT

FANCY GOODS

OPEN ALL NIGHT

❧ STORIES BY PAUL MORAND ❧

Preface by Marcel Proust

Translated from the French by Ezra Pound

EDITED WITH AN INTRODUCTION BY BREON MITCHELL

A NEW DIRECTIONS BOOK

Originally published as *Tendres stocks* (1921) and *Ouvert la nuit* (1922) by Editions Gallimard, Paris.

ACKNOWLEDGMENTS

The editor and publisher acknowledge their indebtedness to the following institutions and individuals for permission to publish relevant material in this volume: The Lilly Library, Indiana University; The Trustees of the Ezra Pound Literary Property Trust; the Beinecke Rare Book and Manuscript Library, Yale University; Donald Gallup; and The University of Virginia Press.

Of the translations in this volume, "Aurora" first appeared in *Antaeus*, "Turkish Night" in *Translation*, and "Borealis" in *Paris Review*.

Manufactured in the United States of America
First published clothbound and as New Directions Paperbook 567 in 1984
Published simultaneously in Canada by George J. McLeod, Ltd., Toronto

Library of Congress Cataloging in Publication Data

Morand, Paul, 1888–1976.
    Fancy goods; Open all night.
        (A New Directions Book)
           1. Morand, Paul, 1888–1976—Translations, English.
    I. Morand, Paul, 1888–1976.   Open all night.   1984.
    II. Title.
PQ2625.067T413   1984   843'.912   83-23705
ISBN 0-8112-0888-5
ISBN 0-8112-0889-3 (pbk.)

New Directions Books are published for James Laughlin
by New Directions Publishing Corporation
80 Eighth Avenue, New York 10011

Contents

Introduction

In the spring of 1976, an elusive and mysterious trunk once owned by **Ezra Pound** was reported to have reappeared at last in Fairfax, Virginia. Rumored to contain a treasure trove of literary letters and manuscripts from his Paris years, the puzzling location of the long-lost trunk was of secondary interest. The exact nature of its contents and the question of ownership were of more immediate concern. If speculations were correct, it held several early drafts of the *Cantos,* as well as other material of central importance to Pound scholarship.

The rumors were true—although the trunk itself no longer existed. The newly discovered translations of Paul Morand's short stories published here for the first time are but part of the riches which came to light as the story of Pound's trunk unfolded. When Pound left Paris for Italy in 1924, scores of his personal letters and manuscripts remained behind at The Three Mountains Press, where he had edited a series of volumes for William Bird, including his own *Indiscretions or Une revue de deux mondes* (1923) and *A Draft of XVI Cantos* (1924). Along with the rest of the books and manuscripts from The Three Mountains Press, the contents of Pound's trunk were retained when Bird ceased publishing and sold out to Nancy Cunard in 1926. The boxes which were in the possession of his grandchildren in Virginia in 1976 had been with Bird when he finally left Paris, first for Chartres, and subsequently for North Africa, where he remained until his death in 1964. From there they made a final journey across the sea to America.

Realizing the importance of the material that had come into their possession, the heirs of William Bird made tentative contacts with local specialists in the rare book trade. Among the handful of major institutional libraries in a position to acquire and house such a collection, the Lilly Library at Indiana University was suggested. There was no need to look further for an interested buyer. A rapid review of the material by William Cagle, the director of the library, revealed a stunning array of letters, manuscripts, corrected proofsheets and proof copies, including the only surviving manuscript of Williams Carlos Williams's *The Great American Novel,* significant runs of previously lost correspondence with T. S. Eliot, Ernest Hemingway, W. B. Yeats, James Joyce, and a lively "war of words" between G. B. Shaw and Pound over the appearance of *Ulysses.* Moreover, the complete publisher's file for Pound's *A Draft of XVI Cantos,* together with original holograph manuscripts and typescripts, had been preserved. Numerous letters from Pound's wife, Dorothy, and other personal papers were also present. In short, it was a scholar's dream.

The next step was straightforward—a professional appraisal of the material by a New York dealer and an offer to buy. It was not long, however, before the matter became more complicated. At Yale University, Donald Gallup, director of the Center for the Study of Ezra Pound and His Contemporaries, who had long been trying to track down Pound's trunk, learned that what looked like his quarry was up for sale. Moreover, the Beinecke Rare Book and Manuscript Library at Yale had a prior claim to the Pound portion of the material, having obtained from Pound's estate the rights to Pound's literary manuscripts and letters as well as to any future finds of a similar nature in the possession of "persons unknown." Gingerly, the two great libraries involved began to discuss the situation, at least in part, through their lawyers. And as wind of the discovery leaked to the press, the *Washington Post* reported: "The puzzle of who owns the important literary property offers an intriguing look at the closed world of academicians and the controversial question of who owns a dead writer's papers."

Within the upper echelons of rare book libraries, such questions are almost always resolved without recourse to litigation. Yale and the Bird heirs were able to reach an amicable solution out of court with regard to the matter of ownership.

Dorothy's letters to Ezra went to their son Omar for an edition of their correspondence. Yale was able to integrate crucial manuscript material from the Paris period into their magnificent Pound collection, while the Lilly Library obtained a score of treasures from one of the major literary finds of the century.

2. POUND AND PAUL MORAND

Paul Morand (1888–1976) was already a force to be reckoned with in Parisian literary circles when Pound arrived in the French capital in 1920. Always ready to champion new and distinct voices, Pound praised a "very divergent group of writers under or about forty years of age, writing without humbug, without jealousy, and without an eye on any market whatsoever." Among them Morand, who offered "the first clear eye that has been able to wander about both ends of Europe looking at wreckage," particularly attracted Pound. Having begun translating Morand as early as 1920, he had signed a contract by the spring of 1922 to translate two volumes of his short stories, *Ouvert la nuit* and *Tendres stocks*.

To his dismay, however, the translations were rejected as "unsuitable for English readers," partly on the grounds of sexual frankness, and in spite of all protestations, the contract was canceled. The typescripts of the stories were returned to Pound, he received a single payment of £25 from the English publishers, and the translations disappeared within the trunk.

Morand, who was elected to the Académie Française in 1968, has remained largely unknown to English-speaking readers, in spite of his immense popularity in the 1920s. To what extent his fortunes might have been improved had Pound's translations appeared, as intended, in the early years of that decade must remain a matter of speculation. English translations which did subsequently appear, "nacherly inferior to mine," as Pound was to report with satisfaction in 1935, seemed unable to maintain the reader's interest, perhaps in part because they were bowdlerized by timid publishers.

Morand's place in literary history rests squarely on his short stories from the '20s. Credited with having introduced a fresh and exuberant style into postwar French letters, he created a series of portraits of young women whom, as Proust pointed out, "we refused to consider as women" before such artists as Renoir, Giraudoux, or Morand brought them to our attention. But what was new in Morand was not simply the whirl of exotic places and sensibilities; it was a singularity of style which joined images in a manner striking and original enough to awaken the admiration of Pound.

Pound had come to Paris in part to renew himself. Having taken leave of London with *Hugh Selwyn Mauberley* (1920), he was, for a time, to turn away from writing poetry, listening instead to the new voices of France. He soon reported: "The 'literary and artistic life' of London having dwindled, the bath of Paris is perhaps unduly pleasant; pleasant, at least, as a matinal cleanliness; hot tub after a fog, and a clean air with a recent vestige of rain."

The following Paris years, until mid-1922, were to constitute what Richard Sieburth has termed "a curious caesura" in Pound's career. But elusive as Pound the poet appears in this period, he was characteristically active. There were, for example, the final stages of his involvement with the gestation and publication of *Ulysses*, with their attendant impact on his own conception of the early stages of the *Cantos*, and his thorough reworking of *The Waste Land* for Eliot late in 1921, two activities alone which serve as milestones in modern literature; there was his increasing interest and interaction with the contemporary avant-garde in Paris, particularly with Picabia and Dadaism; and, as throughout his career, there was his recurrent desire, through translation, to make texts new.

Like Pound, Morand was frequenting Dada and other avant-garde circles in Paris in 1920, while publishing his first poems, most of which dealt with the war and his own experiences abroad in a manner calculated to send at least minor shock waves through the middle class. His short stories, on the other hand, although saturated with a sensitivity which was thoroughly modern and postwar, were still accessible to the public at large.

The son of a richly talented father, the artist and playwright

Eugène Morand, Paul had been sent to England each summer as a young boy to learn English. A year in Oxford at age twenty, followed by a brilliant early career in the diplomatic service, first as an attaché at the French Embassy in London (1913–1916), and subsequently in Rome and Madrid, provided him with a storehouse of experiences and settings which became so intermingled with his art that he later complained of the public's failure to think of him in any guise other than that of a cynical globetrotter, "agité et brutal," always "running after a train, a suitcase in his hand." By the time Pound first contacted him in August of 1920, Morand was serving in the Ministry of Foreign Affairs in Paris and entering into the period generally considered as the most significant and fruitful of his life.

At age thirty-two, and with his major works still ahead of him, Morand must have been flattered to receive Pound's first letters of praise and encouragement. He responded with a copy of his poems *Lampes à Arc* (1919) and a promise to send him even more recent work. *The Dial* was soon to publish one short story by Morand, translated by another hand, and Pound, as their Paris correspondent, was ready to provide them with more.

By November of 1920, Morand had received Pound's first draft of "La nuit turque": "Many thanks for English version of *Turkish Night*. . . . This is very finely put into English. (So used to be stabbed in the back, 'traductore=traditore,' that it is a great pleasure to read something finely written which happens to be one's stuff and some other's too.)" Morand gladly answered Pound's queries, offered several further suggestions of his own, and asked, "Have you got an idea where to give it in England? Many thanks for all the trouble taken."

Pound's revisions reached Morand within a few days, and the French author found himself agreeing with Pound about "the necessity of making an impression on the reader and, if possible, of taking the chance of a knock out. . . . I am sure final version will be quite perfect and it may go to New York at once without my seeing it." "Turkish Night" appeared in the September 1921 issue of *The Dial*, a year in which Morand's literary star was at its zenith. *Tendres stocks* appeared to general praise, and in February of 1922 *Ouvert la nuit* proved an instantaneous success. Proust's introduction to *Tendres stocks* had in Pound's words, "shoveled what one hopes is a final funeral clod upon the corpse of Sainte-Beuve," while at the same time setting the official seal of approval upon Morand and the new generation.

Pound's October "Paris Letter" in *The Dial* brought Morand to the attention of English-language readers again, as one of the standard-bearers of the new prose, "with buddhic eye contemplating the somewhat hysterical war and postwar world and rendering it with somewhat hasty justness. His somewhat unusual title [*Tendres stocks*] may perhaps be translated *Fancy Goods*." While Pound's own admiration for Morand surely included in particular those images which were not "inevitable," he stressed the verisimilitude of the young women's voices: "one has met his ladies '*de par le monde*,' and technically Aurora must be exceeding good, for one can hear the English woman's voice and speech throughout the story, and it cannot be easy to convey these tones of voice and idiom in a foreign speech. Aurora is English, just as Delphine is not English, and in the later stories I think he has sustained his differentiation of nationalities exceedingly well. And he has surely the first clear eye that has been able to wander about both ends of Europe looking at wreckage, and his present news value need not fail ultimately of historic validity." Behind Pound's praise the translator's mind is already at work.

The subsequent story of Pound's abortive attempt to publish translations of both *Tendres stocks* and *Ouvert la nuit* with Chapman and Dodd in England has recently been sketched in Donald Gallup's definitive bibliography of Pound's works. The manuscripts themselves now allow us an even more detailed insight into exactly what happened.

Early in 1922, Pound made contact with a professional translator by the name of Victor Llona, submitting a first draft of "Borealis" ("La nuit nordique") for his comments. Although Llona offered a few gentle criticisms, he termed them "little blemishes in an otherwise excellent piece of work" which "would have disappeared on second reading, anyway." He found "Borealis" a "most cunning title," but feared "the prudery of our Anglo-Saxons will rebel at this naive tale. Here's hoping for a grand scandal."

This reaction must have been music to Pound's ear. By mid-April of 1922, an agreement had been reached with Morand, who was "very glad" to have Pound as a translator. "Generally speaking," he added, "I want to see all the translations before the proofs." Within a month a contract from Chapman and Dodd was available for Pound's signature, and Llona had agreed, at Pound's request, to revise the translation of *Ouvert la nuit* for 400 francs: "Understand I will have nothing to do with the style. Ma suffisance ne va pas jusque là."

The Chapman and Dodd contract was signed on May 22, 1922, with Pound agreeing to provide the manuscript of *Ouvert la nuit* by June 30 of that year and the translation of *Tendres stocks* six months later. For this Pound would receive "world rights" to the translation in the English language and a sum of £120, payable in installments as the two manuscripts were delivered and published. Pound at first took exception to the phrase "suitable for publication in the English language" and noted in the margin: "This to mean that publishers may delete what they think likely to upset Smith & Son and similar pests— for which deletions the translator assumes no aesthetic responsibility." This eventuality was covered in paragraph 3, however, in which the publishers agreed not to make any cuts or alterations in the translation, "except such as shall be essential for the acceptance of the said translation by the ordinary English circulating libraries," and stipulated that any such alterations would be submitted for approval to Morand.

Morand had already extensively revised the English version of "Clarissa" by May 19 but, according to Llona, had no more time "to monkey with the translation" and would soon be returning the remaining scripts in his possession. Llona himself subsequently revised all the stories in draft stage, as agreed, and took over the task of responding to Pound's questions about difficult passages or phrases in the French: "Not the fault of Morand that he hasn't answered your list of queries: I hadn't given it to him. . . . I think I can answer all of them. If not, will ask Morand." The Lilly manuscripts reveal, however, that in addition to "Clarissa," Morand saw and offered suggestions on the final drafts of at least "The Roman Night," "The Six-day Night," and "Borealis." Working steadily on the project, Pound managed to submit the completed typescripts to Chapman and Dodd on schedule in June of 1922.

A record of what happened on the other side of the Channel has been preserved in Guy Chapman's own file now in the private possession of Donald Gallup. Chapman himself was displeased with the translations and sought the advice of an outside reader, turning first to J. Middleton Murry, who had reviewed *Ouvert la nuit* in the *Nation*. Murry was reluctant to accept, pointing out that Morand was a friend and, as an "excellent English scholar," quite capable of evaluating Pound's translation himself. Since Murry was in Switzerland, this lukewarm reception and the possible danger of entrusting the manuscript to the mails led Chapman to try yet another reader, A. B. Walkley, who had reviewed Morand's book for the London *Times*.

"You certainly cannot," he wrote Chapman on August 7, 1922, "with credit, or indeed without ridicule, publish this translation":

> . . . Mr. Pound . . . is literal without tact; he fills in or waters down without taste, often without necessity; he misses, apparently unconsciously, the lilt or rather, the jerk of the author's phrase; he often dulls the edge of the author's sharp epithets. Further he perpetrates some absolute 'howlers,' showing that he does not even understand the author's meaning. There is frequent evidence of sheer carelessness. Lastly, his own style is American, and vulgar American; whereas Morand, though brutal enough, provocative, even slangy, is never vulgar.

Walkley enclosed a two-page list of over twenty specific examples of errors and infelicities from the first twenty-two pages of "Catalan Night." While damning the work as a whole, a few words of faint praise were nonetheless offered: "I have . . . gone through all Mr. Pound's M.S. None of the 'Nights' is, I think, quite as bad as the 'Catalan.' Indeed, the 'Turkish' and the 'Norse' [Borealis] are fairly good, and the 'Six Day' at least shows a remarkable familiarity with American slang."

Walkley went on to question the wisdom of publishing *any* translation of *Ouvert la nuit*: "It is a most piquant performance, delightful to read in the original, but, as we all know, what is piquant in French is apt to become merely coarse in English. The average English reader would miss many of Morand's fine points; but what he wouldn't miss would be such words as 'breasts,' 'thighs,' 'backside,' 'rump.' In short, I think an English version, however accomplished, couldn't fail to be *ugly*." Walkley closed with a postscript: "I assume of course that you will merely take my opinion as a factor in whatever decision you may communicate to Mr. Pound, without naming me—which would serve no useful purpose and would only get me into trouble." This request proved to be a wise one, and it was poor Middleton Murry who wound up as the target of Pound's abusive but misdirected note on August 25: "Toddle on, and take your little dose of arsenic. Devotedly E. P."

Pound was understandably furious that Chapman, who was confirmed by Walkley's opinion in his own assessment of the translations as "quite appalling," wished to back out of the contract, citing in part the "unsuitability" of the texts for English readers. Pound wrote back: "Your letter is an impertinent lie . . . You ordered the translation . . . after seeing . . . Turkish Night, which had already appeared, without causing the least ridicule. . . . There was no question of a verbatim translation into stenographer's pidgeon [sic] English." Pointing out that Morand himself had gone over the translations and approved all changes of idiom and condensation of phrase, he heatedly declared: "If your critics don't yet know that there is a difference between the structure of sentences in English and French, and that conversations have to be translated into speakable phrases, they might do well to learn these primary lessons." Pound threatened legal action, but Chapman was adamant, and a final settlement of £25 was agreed upon, with all rights to Pound's English version waived by the publisher.

Morand himself was obviously embarrassed by the whole affair, particularly in light of the fact that he had indeed reviewed the English versions and approved them and felt a sincere debt of gratitude to Pound. On August 21 he wrote to Chapman asking for details of the affair, "so that I may form an opinion myself before leaving France." On August 24 he thanked Chapman for his "full account" and added somewhat defensively that he had read Pound's second version, which showed "a real improvement," "but . . . I went through it hastily and with imperfect knowledge of English." Morand's first interest remained that of securing an English language edition of his works, and he arranged for a meeting with Chapman later that year in London to discuss other possible translators. It may be safely assumed that this defection put an end to further relations between Pound and Morand, while the latter's willingness to authorize new translations sounded the death knell for any attempt at publishing Pound's for years to come.

Thus ended a literary relationship that might well have remained of continuing importance to both men. There was much in Morand that was attractive to Pound, and it is largely an accident of history that so little attention has been paid to the effect of this period of intense interest in the French writer upon Pound's own work. The rediscovery of Pound's translation now opens the door at last for a closer look.

3. THE TRANSLATION

The stories of Paul Morand offer a unique opportunity to widen our vision of Pound as a translator. We have no other extended example of narrative prose translation from his hand, with the exception of a French novel he cared nothing about and translated anonymously on commission for Boni and Liveright in 1923 and the much shorter first volume of Enrico Pea's *Moscardino* from the early 1940s. While Pound's position as the major creative force in the translation of poetry in our century seems assured, the controversy over the various translations continues, particularly those from classic and Oriental languages. George Steiner's suggestion that "the contemporary translator and even reader of classic verse comes after Pound as the modern painter comes after Cubism" is a "dangerously influential" error in the eyes of Donald Davie, who prefers to believe that Pound's *Homage to Sextus Propertius,* for example, is an intentional "model of how not to [translate]" and claims that Pound "deliberately planted ludicrous howlers, to amuse those who knew the Latin or chose to consult it." Such differences among those who greatly admire Pound's work are mild compared with the steady stream of abuse poured upon the translations by traditional scholars and translators. Pound's *Confucian Odes,* to take yet another now well-known example, are studded with pseudo-etymological readings which admirers find strikingly apt, while to more conservative scholars of Chinese they are simply absurd.

The strength of Pound's achievement as a translator may be measured by the extent to which he has altered our notion of what translation is and can be. Yet it would seem that the justification for his "misreadings" is more easily made in poetry than in prose. The Morand stories thus provide us with significant new material in assessing both Pound's concept of the task of the translator and the complicated interaction between translation and creation in his own works.

The Pound manuscripts in the Lilly Library are richly revealing. They provide a detailed record of the various stages of translation, from first draft through final corrected typescript. Several of the manuscripts also bear the autograph revisions of both Llona and Morand, although Pound always had the final word. It is thus possible to reconstruct, layer by layer, the complex history of the text, which is, in many cases, a history of the interaction of author and translator as well. For the student of translation such a situation is irresistibly intriguing. The sheer volume of the material is such that only a full-length study could do justice to it. Nevertheless, a few general remarks may be ventured.

The aspects of Pound's translation to which A. B. Walkley objected so strongly were, with few exceptions, deliberate choices on Pound's part. The list of errors or infelicities in the first twenty-two pages provided by Walkley includes surprisingly few actual mistranslations. I say surprisingly, since every translator knows that even the best in their trade make mistakes through carelessness or under the pressure of deadlines, and Pound had produced a lengthy manuscript within a relatively short time.

Walkley's objections are what one might expect from a reader unsympathetic to the sort of "knock-out blow" Pound went for on occasion. When Pound translates "dans une atmosphère de tabac" as "in this air freighted with tobacco," Walkley immediately rails, "why depart from the literal, and for the worse?" Walkley's own suggestion ("in an atmosphere of tobacco"), as the manuscript reveals, was in fact Pound's first version, discarded almost before he had written it down. Elsewhere, Walkley objects to Pound for being *too* literal or for Americanisms ("And had him draw up" where Walkley prefers the British "got him to draw up"), accuses him of American prudery (for saying "shirtwaist" instead of "shift," a distinction lost on most readers today), or of falling victim to faux amis (when Pound prefers to translate French "voyage" by "voyage," a "lower-form blunder" in Walkley's eyes). Where Walkley complains of more significant faults, such as a failure to reproduce Morand's rhythmic prose sensitively, his own suggestion seems almost a parody: "Great was my surprise when who should enter but . . ." Pound had offered, "I was considerably surprised when my train companion entered . . ."

This sampling of Walkley's complaints is representative, and it hardly constitutes grounds for breaking a contract. What was really at issue was a matter of tone, the re-creation of the French text in a truly new mode, in short, Pound's whole approach to translation. When Pound prefers "cloaca" to "sewer," Walkley is at a loss ("why the Latin in a book for English readers?"), while for Pound "un beau cloaque" is obviously "a lovely cloaca" and not "a nice sewer." Particularly when the words are placed in the mouth of the story's Spanish heroine. Time and again, Pound translates Morand's dialogue with an energetic freedom which leaves the original phrasing far behind. At times this takes the form of a radical condensation, as when Pound, for example, renders the greeting "Voilà une curieuse rencontre" as "Mm." Pound's ear is always tuned to the colloquial rhythms of actual speech. The opening lines of "Hungarian Night" may serve as a typical example: " 'Give me the long one, that one, with the big hips,' said Jean with boozy insistence." Compare this with the pedestrian English version by Vyvyan B. Holland ("H.B.V.") actually published in 1923: " 'I like the tall one with the big hips,' said Jean, with alcoholic obstinacy." Or consider the reply of the tipsy narrator, choosing his own girl: " 'I like that cross between a unicorn and a red jackass' " in Pound's version, where Holland offered, " 'I like her, she is a cross between a unicorn and a red donkey.' " Similarly striking contrasts between Pound's "unacceptable" version and that finally published in England in the early '20s may be multiplied at will, for both narrative passages and dialogue. One typical example of the former will have to suffice, from the opening of "Aurora." Pound:

> Morning had not yet plumbed the courtyard beneath the open window; above me was the worn sheet-iron sky, bolt-studded with stars, and already acid-stained toward the Orient. A good day for a hanging.

The 1924 English version by H. I. Woolf, with an introduction by none other than A. B. Walkley, offers:

> The window opens on a court, to the depth of which morning is not yet come. Above me, the sky's worn steel-sheet, bolted with stars, and acid stains already in the east. Atrocious morning for an excursion [sic].

Pound's brilliant find for "Atroce matin d'exécution" is just one of the ways in which he manages to remain faithful to Morand precisely by departing from the expected. The reader may judge which version more adequately renders the French: "La fenêtre ouvre sur une cour, au fond de laquelle ce n'est pas encore le matin. Au-dessus de moi, la tôle usagée du ciel, boulonnée d'étoiles, avec des taches d'acide, déjà, à l'orient. Atroce matin d'exécution."

Walkley had accused Pound of prudery, yet he himself feared that any translation of Morand would inevitably be "ugly" because it would include words like "thighs" and "rump." The manuscripts show in fact that Pound translated the stories fully and frankly, without a trace of prudery. Chapman and Dodd were worried about precisely this aspect of the stories. The seriousness of their concern is revealed by the fact that the authorized versions which finally appeared were carefully bowdlerized, a procedure which, at least in the case of "Aurora," vitiated the sense of the story. The version published in 1924 omits the scene in the bath and manages to avoid any indication of nudity throughout the remainder of the tale. The present edition of Pound's translation is thus the first complete and unexpurgated version of Morand's stories available to English readers.

The manuscripts also offer evidence about Pound's attitude toward "mistranslations." On more than one occasion, either Llona or Morand (or both) crossed out a particular word or phrase that was inaccurate; yet Pound, after considering the alternatives, returned to his first choice. Indeed, one is struck by the fact that Pound took over relatively few of the numerous suggestions Morand and Llona made if they had anything to do with style. Even where the author himself was concerned, and taking into account the fact that Morand knew English extremely well, Pound had supreme confidence in his own ability to make the right choice for the English version.

Much more remains to be said about Pound's actual practice in translating narrative prose. But even these brief remarks should indicate that his prose translations reflect the same general aesthetic principles that inform his translations of poetry. These versions of Morand's stories will be open to the usual criticisms, the more so since "Delphine," "Aurora," and Proust's preface have only come down to us in the form of early drafts, with little revision. Nevertheless the confluence here of Pound, Proust, and Morand marks a significant event. Hugh Kenner has noted: "It is because so many Poundian principles meet in the translator's act that the best of his translations exist in three ways, as windows into new worlds, as acts of homage, and as personae of Pound's." For many, these versions may be windows into the new world of Paul Morand. For Pound they were clearly, on one level, an act of homage. It remains to be seen if, and how, Paul Morand might also have offered Pound the opportunity to create yet another of his many personae.

4. A NOTE ON THE MANUSCRIPTS AND THIS EDITION

The aim of this edition is to provide a text of the translation that corresponds as closely as possible to Pound's final intentions. In the case of *Open All Night* we are on fairly firm ground, since Pound himself saw each story through several revisions, and we have the final corrected typescripts as submitted to Chapman and Dodd. *Fancy Goods,* with Proust's preface, presents greater problems. We have only an unrevised draft of the preface, and one of the three stories was taken no further than the uncorrected typescript stage. When *Open All Night* was rejected, *Fancy Goods* was simply put aside. We must assume that Pound would have undertaken further revisions had the project continued.

Because this edition is intended for the general reader, no attempt has been made to provide a scholarly apparatus which would reveal earlier versions or discarded alternative suggestions. In a handful of instances Pound simply left out a word that he could not translate at the moment, obviously intending to fill it in later. Such omissions, as well as a few which were merely typographical, have been rectified in the text and placed in brackets. On the rare occasions when Pound left two possibilities in his own manuscript without any indication as to his final choice, an editorial decision was made between them.

No attempt has been made to correct any "errors" in Pound's translation. Nor have his versions been checked line-for-line with the French originals for accuracy, a task which properly belongs to others. Each story, however, has been carefully compared with the French original with regard to completeness, paragraph division, and the spacing of sections. Pound often deliberately broke up longer French paragraphs, but his autograph drafts are rough enough that innumerable paragraphing errors crept in at the typescript stage. These have been corrected, so that Pound's text now departs from the paragraphing and spacing of the original only when it was clearly intended.

Pound's approach to translation often resulted in the omission of a word or phrase which a more literal translator might have insisted on working into the text. Nevertheless the translation as a whole is complete and comprehensive. The one major omission in the typescript of "Catalan Night" has been restored: an entire page of the original autograph draft was simply left out by the typist. Since it came between two paragraphs, the gap was overlooked by all concerned (except, of course, for A. B. Walkley, who pointed it out in his list of complaints).

Pound was a notoriously poor speller, and his typist in London did not hesitate to correct his errors when she spotted them. Moreover, since the translation was being prepared for publication in England, Pound tried to follow British usage whenever he thought about it. The orthographic results were seldom satisfactory. Pound's punctuation, particularly his comma usage, was also idiosyncratic. Here again his typist seemed to pay little attention, deleting Pound's commas, or adding her own, at random. Pound feared that she would not be able to read his handwriting, and indeed she misread many words that he never caught in proofreading. In the present edition the typescripts have been checked against the autograph drafts for accuracy, spelling errors have been corrected, American orthography has been adopted, and comma usage has been standardized.

All of the autograph drafts are on similar sheets of white, lined paper, folded in half to a page size of 27 x 21.6 cm. Pound wrote only on the front and back of each folded sheet, leaving the inner sides blank. The autograph drafts were then typed, either by Pound or his typist, and further revised. In the case of "Turkish Night," which had appeared in *The Dial,* Pound made his corrections and revisions directly on the tearsheets.

FANCY GOODS

Preface   1. Autograph draft, 27 pp., in black ink, revised only in the process of being drafted, but otherwise uncorrected.

Clarissa   1. Autograph draft, 27 pp., in black ink, revised only in the process of being drafted, but otherwise uncorrected.
2. Typed (carbon) draft, 24 pp., heavily revised throughout in blue ink and pencil by Paul Morand.
3. Typed draft, 24 pp., corrected throughout in black (and sometimes red) ink by Pound, taking over relatively few of Morand's suggestions.

Delphine   1. Autograph draft, 41 pp., in black ink, corrected throughout in red ink by Pound for the typist.
2. Typed (carbon) draft, 27 pp., uncorrected.
3. Typed draft, 27 pp., uncorrected.

Aurora   1. Autograph draft, 42 pp., in black ink, corrected throughout in black ink by Pound, partly revision, partly for the typist.
2. Typed (carbon) draft, 27 pp., uncorrected.
3. Typed draft, 27 pp., revised throughout in blue ink by Pound, with a few corrections in pencil as well.

OPEN ALL NIGHT

Catalan   1. Autograph draft, 72 pp., in black ink, revised through-
Night   out in red ink and blue pencil by Pound, then in black ink by Victor Llona, then again in red ink by Pound.
2. Typed draft, 44 pp., revised throughout in blue ink

and pencil by Pound, and occasionally in black ink by Llona; pp. 28–44 of typescript represent a thorough revision of the autograph draft.

3. Typed (carbon) draft, 44 pp., corrected throughout by Pound, taking over revisions made on the original typed draft (2) and including two or three corrections made after the original typescript was returned from Chapman and Dodd.

Turkish Night

1. Tearsheets from *The Dial* LXXI, No. 3 (Sept. 1921), pp. 281–91, revised throughout in blue ink by Pound, including the insertion of three or four sentences which had originally been omitted. This slightly condensed translation had been prepared in consultation with Morand (see Morand's letters of 10 and 16 November 1920).

The Roman Night

1. Autograph draft, 21 pp., in black ink, revised only in the process of being drafted, but otherwise uncorrected.
2. Typed (carbon) draft, 16 pp., uncorrected.
3. Typed (carbon) draft, 16 pp., revised throughout in black ink by Llona.
4. Typed draft, 16 pp., revised throughout in black ink by Pound, taking into account Llona's suggestions, then revised in blue ink by Morand, then revised again in pencil by Pound in light of Morand's suggestions.

The Six-day Night

1. Autograph draft, 26 pp., in black ink, revised throughout in red ink by Pound.
2. Typed (carbon) draft, 19 pp., uncorrected.
3. Typed (carbon) draft, 19 pp., revised throughout in black ink by Llona.
4. Typed draft, 19 pp., revised throughout in black ink by Pound, taking into account Llona's suggestions, then sparsely corrected and revised by Morand, then revised again by Pound in light of Morand's suggestions, and with a few final corrections by Llona in black ink for the typist.

Hungarian Night

1. Autograph draft, 17 pp., in black ink, revised throughout in red ink by Pound, then in black ink by Llona, with a few final revisions by Pound.
2. Typed draft, 11 pp., varies so greatly from the autograph draft that it constitutes a separate revision by

Pound, revised throughout in blue ink again by Pound, with several corrections of typos by Chapman and Dodd reader.

3. Typed (carbon) draft, 11 pp., in which Pound takes over all changes indicated in the revised typescript (2) prior to submission to Chapman and Dodd.

Borealis

1. Typed draft, 21 pp., uncorrected. Preceded by a no longer extant autograph draft that Llona saw to which he offered corrections (see his letter of April 13, 1922).

2. Typed (carbon) draft, 21 pp., revised throughout in black ink by Pound, then a few revisions in blue ink by Morand, then revised again in pencil by Pound, taking into account Morand's suggestions.

❧ FANCY GOODS ☙

Preface by Marcel Proust

The Athenians are slow in execution. As yet only three young damsels, or dames, have been given up to Morand our Minotaur; seven are specified in the treaty. But the year is not yet over. And many unavowed postulants still seek the glorious destiny of Clarissa and Aurora. I should like to have undertaken the useless labor of doing a real preface for these charming brief romances, which bear the names of these beauties. But a sudden intervention forbade me. A stranger has taken her abode in my mind. She goes, comes, and soon despite her mobility her habits are become familiar to me. And moreover, she has tried like a too long-sighted boarder to establish a personal relation with me. I was surprised at her lack of beauty. I had always thought Death beautiful. How otherwise should she get the better of us? However . . . she seems to be absent for the day, this day. Doubtless a brief absence, if one can judge by what she has left me. There are more prudent ways of profiting by the respite accorded me than to spend it writing a preface for an author already known and who has no need of my prefaces.

Another reason also should have deterred me. My dear master Anatole France, whom I have not, alas, seen for twenty years, has just written in *La Revue de Paris* that all "singularity of style should be rejected." Now it is certain that Morand's style is *singulier*, personal. If I were to have the pleasure of seeing M. France, whose past kindness is still present and living to my vision, I would ask him how he can believe in a unity (or uniformity) of style when men's sensibilities are *singulier* (personal,

3

particular, individual, different one from another). The very beauty of style is the infallible sign that the thought has risen, that it has discovered and knotted the necessary relations of things which their contingence had left separate (inapparent). In *Le Crime de Sylvestre Bonnard* does not the double impression of the wildness and gentleness of cats circulate within the admirable phrase: "Hamilcar, I said to him stretching my legs, prince drowsing in the citadel of the books. [I haven't the work by me.] In this citadel guarded by all the military virtues, you sleep with the softness of a sultana. For you combine the formidable aspect of a Tartar warrior with the heavy grace of female orientals. Heroic, voluptuous Hamilcar . . ." and so on. But M. France wouldn't allow me to say that this page is admirable, because people have written badly since the end of the eighteenth century.

Writing has been poor since the end of the eighteenth century. This gives one food for a multitude of reflections. There is no doubt that many nineteenth-century authors wrote badly. When M. France asks us to abandon Guizot and Thiers to his mercies (the coupling of names is a great dishonor to Guizot) we obey him with joy, and without waiting for the rest of the names, we chuck him all the Villemains and Cousins he desires. M. Taine, with his prose colored like a relief map in order to strike secondary school pupils more vividly, might receive a few honors but can be banished all the same. If we preserve M. Renan because of his just expression of moral verities, we confess that he also writes very badly some of the time. Not to speak of his last works, where the color detonates so constantly that one would think the author had sought a comic effect; nor of his very earliest, strewn with exclamation points, and with a choirboy's constant effusions; the pretty *Origins of Christianity* is for the most part ill-written. One rarely finds so great a pictorial impotence in a prose author of high merit. The description of Jerusalem or Jesus' first arrival is drawn up like a Baedecker: "The constructions vied with the most finished products of Antiquity in their grandiose character, the perfection of workmanship and beauty of the materials. A number of splendid tombs, in original taste . . . etc." Nevertheless, here was a "bit" to "work over," particularly. And Renan thought it his duty to give his "bits" a pomp very much Ary Scheffer–Gounod (we would add also –César Franck if he had written nothing but the solemn, contracted intermezzo of the *Redemption*). To finish a book or a preface with suitable nobility he uses those similes of a head pupil which are in nowise born from an impression: "From henceforth the apostolic bark will fill its sails." "When the overwhelming light had given place to an innumerable army of stars." "Death struck us down both with his wing." And yet during the sojourns in Jerusalem, when Renan calls him "the young Hebrew democrat," and speaks of the "naïvetés" which "this provincial" emits "unceasingly" (How like Balzac!) one asks—as I used to allow myself to ask—if, recognizing thus all the genius of Renan, the *Vie de Jésus* isn't in a way *La Belle Hélène* of Christianity. But M. France mustn't be in too great a hurry for his triumph. We will offer him our ideas about style elsewhere, and someday. Is he quite sure that the nineteenth century was wholly without it?

Baudelaire's style is often external and jolty, but has it ever been equaled as a mere matter of energy? No one has ever written anything less charitable or more vigorous than his verses on Charity:

> A raging angel like an eagle falls from the sky's height,
> In his talons grips the unbeliever's hair,
> And shaking it, he says, shalt know the rule,
> And know that thou must love (make no wry face),
> The poor, the wicked, tortured, and the dolt,
> In order when Christ passes thou mayst spread him
> Triumphful carpet with thy charity.

nor anything more sublime and less expressive of devout souls than:

> Devotion lends them wings and they say to him
> "Lift me, oh mighty Hippogriff, above the skies."

Moreover Baudelaire is a great classic poet and, oddly enough, his classicism of form increases proportionately with the license of his pictures. Racine has written verses more profound but not purer in style than that in the sublime *Poèmes condamnés*. In the poem which caused the greatest scandal:

> Her vanquished arms thrown like vain weapons down,
> All served, and all adorned her fragile beauty.

seem taken from *Britannicus*.

Poor old Baudelaire! begging an article from Sainte-Beuve (with what tenderness, with what deference) and in the end receiving such praises as: "What is certain is that M. Baudelaire gains by being seen. Where one expected the entrance of a strange eccentric, one finds oneself in the presence of a polite, respectful candidate, a nice young man, delicate in language and wholly classic in his forms."

In thanking him for the dedication of *Les Fleurs du mal*, the only compliment he can find is that these pieces give quite a different effect now that they are gathered together. He ends by picking out a few poems to which he applies two-edged epithets, such as "precious" or "subtle," and asks why they aren't written in Latin, or rather in Greek. Fine praise for French verse! These relations between Baudelaire and Sainte-Beuve (Sainte-Beuve, whose stupidity displays itself to the point where one asks whether it isn't a feint or a cowardice) make some of the most heartrending and most comic reading in all French literature.

I once asked myself whether M. Daniel Halévy wasn't joking when he tried, in a superb article in the *Minerve Française*, to melt my heart over Sainte-Beuve's papery phrases, addressed with crocodile tears to Baudelaire: "Ah my child how you must have suffered." Or as thanks, Sainte-Beuve saying to Baudelaire: "I've a mind to scold you . . . you impearl, you petrarchize the horrible. And [I am quoting from memory] one day when we are walking by the seashore, I should like to push you in, and make you swim in full current."

One mustn't pay too much attention to the image itself (which is probably better in its context), for Sainte-Beuve, who knew nothing of these things, had his cynegitic and marine images, etc. etc. He would say "I should like to take [the blunderbuss] and go quickly into the open country to shoot the aimer's gunshot." He would call a book a "picture in etching"; he wouldn't have been able to recognize an etching had you shown it to him. But he found that literature "was very nice," was cute and graceful. But how M. Daniel Halévy (during the 25 years since I last saw him he has not ceased to wax in authority) can seriously think that it is and isn't this great hawker of phrases who "impearls and petrarchizes" rather than the great genius to whom we owe (a thing by no means pearled and petrarch'd, but which seems to me to be fairly well in mid-current):

> For the child in love with maps and engravings
> The universe is equal to his great appetite.
> How vast the world is when the lamps are lit
> And how small the world is in our memory's eye.

It gets thickest when Baudelaire was prosecuted for *Les Fleurs du mal.* Sainte-Beuve didn't want to go into the witness box for him, but he wrote him a letter, which he made haste to ask to have returned to him as soon as he heard of Baudelaire's intention of making it public. Using it later in the *Causeries du lundi,* he felt it his duty to precede it by a little amble (destined to make it still weaker) wherein he says that the letter was written, "in the thought of coming to the aid of the defense." The eulogy was not, however, very compromising. "The poet Baudelaire," he had said, "had spent years extracting from all subjects, and from every flower, a venomous juice, and even, one must say, agreeably venomous. He was moreover an intelligent man, very pleasant, and at times very capable of affection. When he had published *Les Fleurs du mal* he had not thought merely of criticizing, justice was mingled with the critique, as if there really was a danger of hidden malices and meanings in the elegant rhymes" (all of which in parenthesis doesn't so much accord with "my child you must have suffered"). Moreover in this scheme for his own defense Sainte-Beuve speaks well of an illustrious poet ("Far be it from me to diminish in any way the glory of an illustrious poet, of a poet dear to all of us, and whom the emperor deemed worthy of a public funeral"). Unfortunately this poet thus finally glorified isn't Baudelaire, it is Béranger. When Baudelaire, on the advice of Sainte-Beuve, withdrew his candidature for the academy, the great critic complimented him and imagined he was filling his cup of happiness by saying: "When they read your last phrase, conceived in such modest and polished terms, they said aloud, 'Very well.'" The most terrifying part is not only that Sainte-Beuve thinks he has been very good to Baudelaire, but alas that in the complete dearth of encouragement, or of the soberest justice accorded him, Baudelaire shares the critic's opinion, literally does not know how to show his appreciation to the latter.

However enthralling this story of genius not understanding itself, we must tear ourselves from it to come back to the question of style. It certainly hadn't the same importance for Stendhal that it had for Baudelaire. When Beyle had offered a landscape, "these enchanting spots," "these ravishing places," or to one of his heroines "this adorable woman," "this charming woman," he desired no greater precision. He lacked it, in fact, to the point of saying "she wrote him an infinite letter." But if one considers that the great unconscious bony structure underlying an assemblage of ideas is a part of style, then Stendhal had it. What pleasure I should have in showing that each time Julien Sorel or Fabrice quit the vain cares to live a disinterested voluptuous life, they do so always in a high place (whether it is Fabrice's prison or Julien's in Abbé Banès' observatory). This is as beautiful as the deliverers of salutations, analogous to new angels, who here and there in Dostoevsky's writings bend down to the very feet of him whom they think they have assassinated.

There Beyle was a great writer without knowing it. He considered literature not only below life, of which it is, on the contrary, the terminus, but below the stalest diversions. I confess that if it were sincere nothing would scandalize me more than Stendhal's: "Some people arrived and we did not leave till quite late. The nephew had some excellent zambaglione sent in from the Café Pedroti. In the country where I am going, I said to my friends, I am not likely to find a home like this, and to pass the long evening hours I will do a novel on our amiable Duchess Sanseverina." *La Chartreuse de Parme,* written for the lack of houses where one conversed pleasantly and where they served zambaglione, is in fairly complete opposition to the single alexandrine toward which tend, according to Mallarmé, the divers vain activities of the life universal.

"No one has known how to write since the end of the eighteenth century." Isn't the contrary equally true? In all the arts, it seems that talent is the artist's approach to the object to be expressed. As long as the distance between them subsists, the job isn't finished. This violinist plays his violin phrase very well, but you see his effects, you applaud, he is a virtuoso. When all this has disappeared, so that the violin phrase shall be one with an artist wholly melted into it, the miracle will be accomplished. In other centuries, it seems that there always was a certain distance between the object and the highest minds that discoursed about it. But in Flaubert, for example, the intelligence, which may not have been of the greatest, tried to make itself into the shaking of a steamboat, the color of moss, an island in the bay. Then there comes an instant when one no longer finds the intelligence (even the moderate intelligence of Flaubert), one has before one the moving boat "meeting the trail of logs which begin to undulate in its wake." This undulation is the intelligence transformed, incorporated in the matter. It succeeds also in penetrating the heather, the beeches, the silence and light of the underbrush. The writer's first effort toward style ought to be just this transformation of energy where the thinker disappears, and which carries the things before us.

But M. France disagrees: "What is your canon?" he asks of us in this article which starts off André Chaumeix' new *Revue de Paris* with such gusto. And among those whom he proposes to us, and in comparison to which we write badly, he cites Racine's *Lettres aux imaginaires*. We refuse the very principle of a style unique and independent of multiform thought. But, in the end if we had to choose one (and one which, as M. France means, should not be a heavy cannon) we would not choose, not ever, the *Lettres aux imaginaires*. Nothing so dry, so impoverished, or so short. A form in which so little thought has been put might easily be light and graceful. But that of the *Lettres aux imaginaires* isn't: "I would even believe, if you will, that you are not of Port-Royal, as one of you says. . . . How many people have read his letter who would not have regarded it had not Port-Royal adapted it, had not these gentlemen distributed, etc." "Ye think to say, for example, something mightily agreeable when ye say of an exclamation which M. Chamillard hath made, that his great O is only an o in cipher . . . one sees soon that ye but force yourselves upon pleasantry." True these repetitions would not stop the impetus of one of St. Simon's paragraphs, but here, where is the onrush, or the poetry, or even the style? Really these letters to the author of the *Imaginaires* are almost as feeble as the silly correspondence in which Racine and Boileau exchange their opinions on medicine. Very unmedical. Boileau's snobbism (rather what we should find today in a government clerk's excessive deference to officialdom) is such that he prefers Louis XIV's advice (which Louis was sensible enough not to give) to that of the doctors. He is persuaded that a prince who has succeeded in taking Luxembourg is "inspired by heaven" and can emit only "oracles," even in medicine. (I am sure that in their very justifiable admiration for the Duc d'Orleans, my masters MM. Léon Daudet and Charles Maurras and their delightful follower Jacques Bainville wouldn't go to the point of asking his medical advice at a distance.) "Moreover," adds Boileau, "who wouldn't be happy to the point of losing his voice and speech at hearing that the king had asked for news of him."

It is no use saying that this was part of the age, and that the epistolary style was always like that. Without going very far, any further indeed than a certain Wednesday (presumably in December) of 1673, that is to say, just midway between the *Imaginaires,* written in 1666, and the *Lettres* of Racine and Boileau (1687), Madame de Sévigné wrote from Marseilles: "I am charmed with the individual beauty of the city. Yesterday, the weather was heavenly, and the place from which I looked out at the sea, the cliffs, the mountains and the city is amazing. The crowd of knights who came yesterday to see M. de Grignan on his arrival, known names, Saint-Herem etc.; adventurers, swords, hats, with a manner; people made to illustrate an idea of war, of romance, of embarkment, of chance, of chains, slave's irons, servitude, captivity, for me who love romances it was all an enchantment." Admitted that this isn't one of Mme de Sévigné's letters as I best like them. But in spite of everything, in her composition, her coloring, her variety, what a picture for a "French tribune" in the Louvre this great writer has painted us. Such as it is, in its magnificence, I dedicate it to a man to whose family Mme de Sévigné was so proud (she repeatedly says so) of being related through the Grignans, my friend the Marquis de Castellane.

Beside such pages the meager correspondence of which we were speaking counts very little; which doesn't prevent Boileau's being an excellent poet, sometimes delightful. And doubtless in Racine an hysteric of genius was struggling in the control of a superior intelligence, and acts for the latter in his tragedies, with a perfection that has never been equaled, the flux and reflux, the multiple reiterated beat, and the passion, totally seized despite all this. All the avowals (withdrawn as soon as she feels they are ill received, reiterated, as one fears, against all evidence that they have not been understood, aggravated up to a flagrance without equivocation, after so many sinuous detours) which so inimitably vitalize the scene in *Phèdre,* and cannot but leave us, retrospectively, surprised and by no means charmed in the presence of the *Lettres aux imaginaires.* If we must absolutely adopt a canon of the sort that one can extract from these *Lettres,* we would much rather, sometime or at once (accepting M. France's view that no one can write nowadays) take the preface (on his status of half-madness) which Gérard de Nerval dedicated to Alexandre Dumas: "They [his sonnets] would lose their charm by being explained, if the thing were possible; grant me at least the merit of the expression; the last madness to remain with me will probably be the mania of thinking myself a poet, it is up to criticism to cure me." Very well, if one is going to take the *Imaginaire* as a canon of something well written, here is something written better; but we don't want a "canon" of any sort. The truth (M. France knows it better than anyone, for he knows everything better than anyone else) is that from time to time a new and original writer arrives (call him if you like Jean Giraudoux or Paul Morand, since for some reason unknown to me, people are always bringing Morand and Giraudoux together like Natoire and Falconet in the marvelous *Nuit à Châteauroux,* without their having any resemblance). This new writer is usually fatiguing to read and difficult to understand because he joins things by new relationships. One follows the first half of the phrase very well, and then one falls. One feels it is only because the new writer is more agile than we are. New writers arrive like new painters. When Renoir began to paint people did not recognize the objects he presented. Today it is easy enough to say that he is an eighteenth-century painter. But in saying it one omits the time factor, and it needed a great deal of time, even in the nineteenth century, to have Renoir recognized as a great artist. To succeed, the original painter, the original writer, proceeds like an oculist. The treatment—by their painting, their literature—is not always agreeable. When they have finished they say: "Now look!" And there it is, the world which has not only been created once, is created as often as a new artist arrives, appears to us—so different from the old one—perfectly clearly. We adore the women of Renoir, Morand, or Giraudoux, whom before the artist's treatment we refused to consider as women. And we want to walk in the forest, which on the first day had looked to us like anything you like, except a forest—for example a tapestry with a thousand nuances, and lacking exactly the nuances of forest.

Such is the perishable, new universe which the artist creates and which will last till a new artist appears. To all which many things might be added. But the reader who has already suspected them will define them better than I could in reading "Clarissa," "Aurora," and "Delphine."

The only reproach I might be tempted to offer Morand is that he uses images other than the inevitable images. No, all the "almost" images among images don't count. Water, in given conditions, boils at 100° centigrade. At 98° or 99° the phenomenon does not occur. In which cases he would do better to do without images. Take someone who does not know Wagner or Beethoven, put him at a piano for six months, let him try all the combinations of notes that chance offers him, the spring theme of the Valkyrie or the pre-Mendelssohn, or rather infinitely super-Mendelssohn of the fifteenth Quatuor will never be born of his hammering. While Péguy was alive, they reproached him for trying to say a thing in ten ways when there was only one way of saying it. The glory of his death has wiped it all out.

It seems as if our minotaur Morand had up to the present searched the detours of his "vast retreat," as Phèdre calls it in the scene I have referred to—in French and foreign palaces, built by architects inferior to Daedalus. From whence he watches the young ladies in dressing gowns, with sleeves fluttering like wings, young ladies who have had the imprudence to descend into the labyrinth. I know these palaces no better than he does, and would be of no use to him in solving their shrouded and fractious mystery. But if, before becoming an ambassador, or rivaling Consul Beyle, he will visit the Hôtel de Balbec, I might endeavor to lend him the fatal thread:

> "Tis I, my prince, tis I whose useful aid
> Hath taught you the wrong turnings of the labyrinth."

Clarissa

In Memory of E. B.

✑ I knew you, Clarissa, in the happy days. And those days, so easily filled by our minuscule occupations, recall your glass cabinets, too small to hold the vain and costly knickknacks on which you spent your affection. We met at night in the most lit, most sonorous houses where there was dancing. Sleep carried me well along into the days and often the telephone woke me.

"Look out of the window, I am sending you a fine cloud."

I would hardly have time to hang up the receiver—for we lived near each other. I would run barefoot to the window and watch the gray or pink mass approaching along the skyline, heavy and sluggish with its freight of welcome.

I would hurry to take you out—that is, the winter afternoons are short—to haggle over a useless bit of silk with a secondhand dealer in Ebury Street—late arrivals, in the shop already full of shadow, with a loitering last glow on lacquers and steel armor and on the dealer's false teeth that you joked about.

Those were, I mean, happy days: the days.

When I engulf myself in their memory, two visions emerge.

Night, clear night, isolated in a spring full of rain, and still exhaling the warm blue clarity of the rain. The windows are open, and we have our elbows on the rail of the balcony. You lean out to sniff the smell of the fresh-cut grass that comes up from Kensington Gardens and mixes with the animal perfume of the dance; the acid green of your Longhi cloak weighs heavily against the background: the brilliant orange of an arched Japa-

13

nese bridge. The masks are crowding her against the parapet, this woman on the bridge with naked breasts who laughs and throws bread crumbs to the carp. The black falling Venetian headdress shut in your face with its shadow, showing only a curious mouth, chemical red. The night shut in all the fête likewise with fat velvety darkness, pierced only by the wheels of the inverted Wain which fell vertically upon us in its lasting immobile fall.

Next: day in the country.

The tennis court seems to have been cut into the truncated hilltop from which the county like a useless expensive park fell away to the sea in soft undulations. A young man in white ducks receives with a long slow stroke, gathering his shadow and his movement into a sort of disc at his feet. On the mound of bluish grass, girls in knitted golf jackets, cerise, yellow, green, cerise, are gathered around a rattan tea table. And the center of all this lightness, this so highly shined pleasure, the luminous node of this circle of women, themselves framed in the vaster circle of sky and country, is the silver teapot, burbling like a lot of wasps over a tart, its lid reflecting the sky in convex, the tree shadows, its ribbed sides giving off delicately distorted figures, and narrow strips of color for the knitted jumpers, cerise, yellow, green, and cerise.

Abstract oneself from the present, an instant, and how?

A stretch of mud with grass sprouting on it so that the whole looks like a sponge wrapped in a moldy, green twilight; nothing limits it save the sky, and some sheds to the left, built in unpainted white wood, and conveying to me the odor of rancid butter. Puddles of water throw up to the washed and empty sky the image of its aluminum moon. On the dilapidated roads the faceted wheels of heavy artillery have left vertebrate tracks now full of mauvish water.

Again: the fenced, soggy road between the arsenal and the barracks, the infantrymen in their tunics. Caissons jolt along in the mud under the low-lying heaven, dray horses pull at the traces, urged on by soldiers with soft expressionless faces. Behind them the plain slopes to the lead-colored river and is covered with a multitude of tents, carts, marine guns without carriages, streaked with ridges of violet earth, regular as moles' tracks—the trenches of the New Army.

Finally, against the sky, the aligned chimneys, the squat city gas reservoirs, the bridges of latticed iron, the bright rails, signal discs, masts of sailboats, the heavy smoke of ships with steam up, and the arsenal dipping its pink steps in a river full with the flood tide.

You don't believe in the war. You say:
"In any case it won't last long."
"It would be too awful. . . ."

Or:

"It's impossible, I know Munich."

But the Germans made war on France in order to come to the Café de Paris in uniform. They made war on England because they believed British tailors gave them bad fits on purpose.

When I telephoned you that Germany had declared war on Russia, you answered:
"I was in the garden, cutting roses . . ."

The thought of all your relatives, of your friends in France, made you anxious, but you could not free yourself from the sense of security which people have when they live in a place surrounded by water.

This country awoke to the war, slowly. The realization drifted in from outside, from seeing the German Jews in Commercial Road putting up their shutters; those in the West End hiding their pictures; from the fall in consols in London, the drop of wool prices in Sydney, the Americans taking flight in their nickel-plated touring cars, and gold, oh gold much more timid; arthritic diplomats left the watering places, you learned, without having finished their cures, kings "regained" their capitals, other countries bolted their frontiers. Then the departure of the

15

French cooks and barbers, they went down to the station with a flag.

Warships sailed out of Portsmouth as in other years for the regattas, only their guns were unmuzzled, and the German yachts didn't come. The sea reacted first, then the coasts, the coast guards mounted the semaphores with their baggage wrapped in green cloth. The fever worked in gradually toward the center. All imperceptibly. England knew nothing of that sleepless August night when millions of men kissed their wives with dry lips, and burnt their letters. She did not hear the clatter of clearing the decks, she didn't clamp her portholes, did not cut loose her anchors.

They put a policeman on duty outside the German Embassy, S.W.1.

When that had been understood they built barracks.

Could they have done anything different in an unwounded country, where the children have never found bullets from earlier wars stuck in the walls of their houses?

Would you expect the streets to empty themselves at a given signal? Gowned lawyers, footmen in amaranth liveries, judges in wigs and robes, bookmakers in mastic overcoats with pearl buttons going on foot to the stations, going to interior garrisons, peers guarding bridges over which no crowded trains were yet moving toward our frontier?

I hear you coming, Clarissa. You walk on your heels, with long, decided steps, there is no whispering of silk skirts, you are a whistling ragtime.

You are tall, broad-shouldered, a good face and red hair. You are not proud of your beauty, but you like your hair to be noticed. You say:

"I adore redheads. I always notice an auburn."

You reject the indirect compliments which brunettes fish for, when they profess that only blondes are charming.

You say, "I'm redheaded, and I have a bad temper, like every other redheaded woman."

You are not, at first go, sympathetic, especially when one meets you for the first time in society, without your house, without your friends, without your explanatory periphery, in a hat, with your gloves on. You look round severely, shut your lips, straighten your back, and seem to say to everyone else: "I am taller than you are!"

And you are so badly dressed. In a sort of good way. Your shoes are pointed, and one expects them to have flat heels; your dresses are simple, the skirts short and with pockets; you wear them for a long time, and from morning till evening. One supposes that your toilet is finished when you get out of your bath— when you have cleaned yourself. You get up at seven, go down to breakfast, fully dressed, at eight. You tuck stray locks of hair under your hat, in the carriage.

When I comment on it, you say:

"I haven't time. There are things more interesting . . ."

This indifference isn't a pose, for one occasionally discovers concessions to fashion (especially in your evening dresses)—and wishes you hadn't made them.

Not that you don't know what's being worn, for you design dresses for others, and you like to have women amusingly gowned, and well-dressed young men about you.

I have at times succeeded in making you give up a style fifteen years old for one thirty years old. And when you want to be nice to me, you do your hair in a fringe, and put a black velvet riband round your neck "à la Degas."

From the first day I was curious about you, very. I have stayed so. Only your indocile temper has kept me from falling in love with you.

Your face is interesting. There is a great mystery in your set lips, a good deal of sensuality in your nose with its mobile large nostrils, and an attraction in your yellow eyes, generally rather hard, yielding at moments, and bounded by the mauve vein which shows through the skin at their corners.

You know a good deal without being cultivated. You know nothing of history, and understand the past better than the savants when you handle an old slipper or an old bit of embroidery.

Books you do not like. I have never seen you with a novel. In your library there are engravings, documents, catalogues. That is all.

I know that you will never grow old, will never come to an end. When I feel like dying I call on you during your toilet. You don't interrupt it, you go on polishing your nails, or tying your bootlaces; you exclaim:

"To live!" You say, "I am alive, my friend, that's enough. To be able to run, to stop, to be ready, to be tired, to be able to spit, to spit into the fire, into water, to spit out of the window onto the heads of the bystanders, very fine, very fine all of it."

And you are really like that: you enjoy your health. The beat of your pulse, the use of your limbs, all these pleasures, negative for the rest of us, you take with a sort of lucidity; you move your arms with the pleasure anyone else would have if they, the arms, were to be amputated in an hour. You use your legs with the joy a paralytic would have in regaining the power of movement. You take possession of a room, or of a sidewalk, as if they had been for a long time forbidden you. Alone by your sole self unsupported you give the impression of a popular holiday, of a crowd from boxed narrow streets, released, lying over a greensward like the washing.

Life's so twisted into you that it would take great effort to get it away from you. Dentists would pull in vain at your teeth, and not shake one. You are never ill. You survive even English doctors.

I find Clarissa in her sitting room, hands and face black, and her clothes dust-covered. She says: "I'm arranging things."

Clarissa says that she likes empty spaces, bare walls, polished floors reflecting the walls, and cleared tables. But she succumbs, victim to her predilection for trinkets. She obeys the successive solicitations of form, color, sentiment, and the cabinets, shelves, mantelpiece are insufficient; without her knowing it the bibelots get stuffed into wooden chests, under the furniture; the drawers will no longer shut, even the entrance into the room becomes difficult . . . or improbable. Then Clarissa reacts; there is a parting in sorrow, the beloved truck is removed, exiled to the attic, where she discovers it, years later, and drags it out again— for a season.

By day, and all day, she ransacks suburban antiquaries, Hebrew hand-me-downs, old-clothes dealers. She goes with her long stride, and gripping a basket, to the old iron market, regardless of fleas; she wheedles the vendors, pokes about with ragpicker's flair, and comes home with her pockets and muff full of new rubbish. She likes them all, from the really rare to the bolts, doorknobs, nails, and old pennies.

She says: "I am like a magpie." Like a magpie she seizes bright objects and hides them in places known only to herself, chucked in pell-mell with other objects found in the street. When are you going to take to shoplifting, Clarissa? Her bedroom is full of colored glasses, broken bottles, carafe stoppers, crystals, scraps of luster or of mirrors, and animals in blown glass.

"How nice it all is to touch!"

And she strokes the corners and surfaces, she holds them up against the light, near the window, and enjoys their refractions. One recognizes her balcony from the street by the globes of crystal; she hangs glass balls from her ceiling, and they hold the whole street in multiform truncated image; the clouds revolve slowly in them, and the motorbuses at quick time.

Clarissa keeps a close eye on the auction rooms, all of them.

There is in London no single great market where everything that is for sale changes hands daily. There are a series of dealing places, each with its physiognomy, its habits, its public. It is a social hierarchy rather than a mere difference of quarter. Clarissa sees in it only a difference in distance, purely spatial.

She will start with the ostentatious, the places with monumental stairs, and liveried porters, where they sell museum pieces, the remnants of royal ruin, marginalia of immense estates, with decorated art experts and titled critics looking on.

A few blocks away are in the caricature of these rooms. The same porters—a bit older, with threadbare liveries; exhibitions of anonymous masters, indecent Rembrandts, Corots without shame, selling to touts and cheats in all ambiguity.

Other places specialize in jewels; gold ornaments are handed round to dirty Armenians with black wool beards, and the Jews sniff over the pearls.

She goes also to popular sales, where small war profiteers seize on pianos, panoplies, music boxes, Indian carpets in coarse wool, plated ware, and plush armchairs.

At times she mounts to the source, i.e., docks, where the boats from the Far East dump out their cargoes and sell on the spot at auction.

But her preference is for county sell-ups, where the whole contents of a house is turned out from wine cellar to door latches, and her flair guides her, accurately, across these shipwrecks of life, through these demolitions of objects.

Clarissa does not acquire things without remorse. She has reasons, each time, for the purchase.

"It will be a good wedding present; instead of giving an atrocity . . ."

"The children need it . . ."

"It's not for me, it's a commission."

"I let one go by last year, just like it, you can't find them anywhere, any longer . . ."

Clarissa buys something in memory of every pleasure, as a memento; she buys something to help her forget every sorrow, something small.

I might catalogue Clarissa's love for old costumes, half-open her chests of antique shoes, dolls, marionettes, dig up the embroidered waistcoats, fancy dress, military uniforms, theater properties, gay rags, scraps, tatters, a mass of truck that even a taste for antiques couldn't by any possibility excuse, but I still shouldn't have given more than a glimmer of what I am trying to explain.

She laughs in showing them.

"Things of no possible use."

Worse. Little unimaginable trifles, without age, never twice looked at, the museum of an infant savage, curiosities of a lunatic asylum, the collection of an anemic consul come back from the tropics.

She confesses:

"You know my tastes: broken mechanical toys, burnt milk, steam organs, the smell of priests, black silk-flowered corsets, and bouquets of colored beads representing all the flowers mentioned in Shakespeare . . ."

The deliria of *Une Saison en enfer* come suddenly into my mind.

"I love the idiot paintings, scenery for cheap theaters, trappings to go, pictures of acrobats, shop signs . . ."

Still more odd is her taste for fake. She likes the sham thing better than the real. She enjoys her own disappointment and yours. When she sees women looking at her pearls, she's amused at arousing so much low passion at so little expense. She loves that paraphrase of the true, the modern religion of sham, the irony latent in the fake, the satire of nature, the showing up of it as useless and imperfect. She likes to disguise herself. She spots her silks, dyes her carpets, discolors her hair, paints her cats. She has around her innumerable things used for what they weren't intended, books that open as boxes, penholders holding a spyglass, chairs which turn into tables, tables which turn into screens, to say nothing of the jack-in-the-box jewelry that we owe to Italian and Japanese bad taste.

The cheap suburban jewelry shops with their false stones and filigree fascinate her. She does not want panther-skin but can't keep her eyes off the grossest imitation of it—black spots on sand-colored rabbit.

She puts glass fruit and crystal pears into great bowls, but she really reserves her tenderness for this sort of thing: oranges shining with sticky varnish, celluloid cherries, vitreous grapes, overswollen, with sickly undersized leaves. She doesn't care for dwarf cedars until they are dead. Then she can paint them with red lacquer and make them sprout petals of silver paper and pistils of feathers.

"I am planning an artificial garden," she said. "It will be in the middle of a park. One will get there quite naturally as if one were coming into the coolest and shadiest spot, and then find a sterilized vegetation. One can stretch out on that lovely green that you only get in dyed moss, and feel its warm, dusty surface. There will be borders of colored beads, flowers of silk paper, under glued cloth leafage, and gutta-percha carp will swim in the melted glass of the pool . . ."

Clarissa has a town house and a country house. Our life swings from one to the other like a pendulum, they share the year unequally; one having the rapid compact months of winter, the other the transparent summer months. They are not far apart. From the terrace of the town house you can see the country house on the blue line of hills which bounds London like the bent lip of a cup.

The town house has a noble and privileged air. Byron lived in it. It keeps its place, it respects the alignment of sidewalk and skyline. The lines of its façade are of a severity which would bore one, but for the thought of the thousand excesses behind them.

The other house is small, and precocious, like a bit of Empire furniture left out in the garden. Its center is scooped out by a round hall with a balcony onto which all the rooms open, so that the guests can throw apples into the rooms opposite before they are out of bed in the morning . . .

Apart from the two Persian cats who sleep by the fireplace, rather as if they were piles of its ashes, Clarissa has few intimate friends.

As you like, Clarissa, let us talk, of your friends, my companions.

You are the center of a very small world which seems to have no raison d'être but yourself. We could no more imagine any other sort of life than this which you thrust upon us than could your bibelots. (For you do impose things. You are a large woman, with decisive gestures, with a definite visage, strong lungs and having the air of authority.)

You do not say: "What shall we do this evening?"
You say: "We are going to the Alhambra, Box 6."
We are your prisoners. Everything carries us back to you. Boredom, if we are distant; if we go down your street, the big flat pleasant-feeling bell button attracts us, everything attracts us; the noise of our steps on the marble stairs, the parrot's insults, the odor of transfer paper and palettes which comes from your boudoir, the cameo in your signet ring, the mauve veins tinting your eyeballs.

There is no bond between the lot of us, save yourself, but we have a certain family likeness. We are all slender, young, and with bright eyes and red lips. We laugh loudly, take our drinks neat, never get up for breakfast in the morning, dance fandangos across the house, and know enough to keep quiet when you play the piano.

You like to bring us together, you know nothing of jealously isolated friendships, but you distinguish some particular quality in each one of us, and like him or her on account of it, sic: Pamela, mahogany hair; Tom, slender wrists; Rafael, a pretty face and a knack for the banjo; as for me, I, as you say, go well with your Chinese room.

We are here round a table at Murray's, for our common pleasure, i.e., hers. Clarissa dominates us all by her height, she is a more brilliant object than the women, she has more assurance than the men; the waiter naturally goes to her for the orders. We gather about her, happy to be in this comfortable cellar, in these adorned catacombs, pleasure ruling. The downstairs women have their nails polished, their faces well painted, and their armpits are visible. Couples revolve about an imaginary axis, wringing the waltz as if it were a wet rag out of which a melody had to be squeezed. The downstairs men have one arm in a sling, or a bandaged head; the Negro music tires them rather, or brings them back against the ineffaceable memory of a trench where they were hit, or of the first glass of water. The waiters stumble over crutches that are lying about on the floor.

There are also fatter more flourishing males, drinking Pommery out of older bottles, it is after ten o'clock. They are neutral. They are Scandinavians, Dutch, and Americans. They blink at each other; offer two hundred thousand Mausers to be delivered at sea off Barcelona (quietly). They undo their revolver pockets and take out cloth samples for uniforms of all the belligerent armies. They buy rejected lots, good-humoredly (get 'em off on the Russians), and they take up delayed contracts. The hurricanes of shot go out of this night club and will burst sooner or later. Tom grins at it.

"Dernier cri. Yes, very, last cry of the sufferers."

He offers one of them a bit of shrapnel removed recently from his head, saying:

"If you can use it over again . . . ?"

There are five of us round a small table with plates and elbows crowded together. Pamela is muffled up in her ermines, silent, her eyes tired by the stage light, rouge still on her cheeks, looking poorly. She eats her eggs and bacon, lights an amber-perfumed cigarette, and unfolds suddenly like a camelia, her cloak slipping down over her arms. Narrow shoulders, built, as Rafael says, like a soda bottle. She is in grief. She says:

"I can't keep a cook."

Tom's left eardrum is still at La Bassée, he lifts his hand to his good ear to hear better, takes her remark for a joke, grins, thereby wrinkling his cheeks chapped bright in the Flanders wind.

Rafael orders a large supper and eats phlegmatically. His kid's face (Transvaal decoration) looks eighteen and is perfectly calm; he is set there in the midst of the agitation as he always has been in the middle of his own absurdly quotidian, wholly unstable existence. He is systematic lunacy. One feels that he has no tie to the rest of the world. Without obligations, without troubles, without domicile, without bank account, without anything but the jewels he is wearing. No symptom of his past is apparent; the nights of pleasure in Montmartre, in Rome; the nights of gambling at Deauville; dancing nights at St. Mortiz; of love in Poland, or Madeira, have slid off him, have flowed over his polished face leaving no mark.

Neither insolent nor obsequious, he moves through life an indolent animal *de luxe,* and with—like other old Etonians—the somewhat affected mannerisms of a flirt who doesn't like work.

Clarissa has him about like a good-looking cat; like a cat he expects and gets infinite consideration for the kindnesses he consents to receive—he tempers dependence by an affectation of indifference.

Clarissa watches him eat.

Now and again Louise comes to us between dances. She is pretty, in an inedible sort of way, which gives us no particular pleasure. She has no dazzle and goes dull on approaching us.

Louise wants to talk, her eyes revolve slowly (she must have been brought up near a railway line where they ran no express trains); her mouth opens. She produces: "I . . ."

Rafael interrupts her. She shuts her mouth, opens her handbag, looks into it as if into the depths of a well; then cigarette case, holder, a cigarette, cotton, a lighter; then powderpuff, rough; she redoes her surface.

She is going to speak, her mouth again forms an oval; she says: "I . . . eh . . ."

She is so startled that she doesn't go on with it. She wipes off her excess eyeblack. She reflects.

"This war's a bore. It must be very boring in the trenches. The dentist's another bore. I spent two hours at the dentist's this morning; talk about neuralgia this evening. To think it took me twenty years to learn what a toothache is like. I wanted to have this one filled, no, this one, the back molar . . ."

She arouses only a courteous interest. With us her assurance fails her. She sees Clarissa, whose eye appears to be saying:

"You never will understand."

She gets up and goes to show her back tooth to the Duc d'Orléans, who places his finger on the cavity.

It is four o'clock. We ascend to the earth's surface, leaving beneath us the heavy cigar smoke and the odors of jicky and foie gras. It is still night outside, the blackened and shaded streetlights drop furtive, half-luminous circles as if from stationary dark lanterns; a policeman is trying the doors; two dustmen are reading the French communiqué by the glimmer of a lantern.

I suggest a taxi, Clarissa prefers returning on foot.

She says, "Take my arm. I love the night so. Why should we swamp half of our priceless life in slumbers? Why did they send us to bed so early when we were children, on the pretext that night isn't made for children? Did you get up at night? Tell me?"

"Yes, Clarissa. After my mother had kissed me and tucked me in, I used to get up again. My window opened on the balcony on the street. That balcony was great fun. I can still feel the sun-warmed lead under my bare feet. The sun stayed on it till evening; I still have on my tongue the fresh taste of the iron railing that I used to lick; I had planted nasturtiums in boxes that they had filled for me with real earth bought in the Cours-la-Reine market. Through the next window I could see my father in the gloom of the studio. He drew standing, I could see the easy sweep of his fine pale hand in the circle of lamplight. A gray violet July evening came down on tender and languid Paris. Horses scraped the stable floors with their shod feet, concierges smoked in the calm air at the doors, the Eiffel Tower had not yet her Marconi-wave collars but wore an emerald on her forehead, footmen drank the liqueur dregs in cocottes' apartments, and the latter were visible, at the end of the street, in muslin, going up the Champs Élysées toward the Arc de Triomphe, in coupés drawn by pink horses. The sun went to bed in Neuilly, and they dined at the Châlet du Cycle."

Clarissa tightens her grip on my arm, she takes my hand.

She says: "That's it. Just like me. I have the same blood, it runs in my veins like warm wine on cold mornings; I have the same fits of nerves that you get on stormy evenings. We are very near to each other."

"Very near, Clarissa. It's a duet, and we touch each other. Our thoughts walk in step beside each other. In the street our eyes light at the same instant on a funny hat feather, our curiosity on the same bodice . . ."

I was going to show you this decorated Frenchman, with his pants unbuttoned, washing his hands with imaginary soap . . . but you have long since caught sight of him.

You say:

"Frenchmen's faces are like a room with too much in it. One finds mustaches, a beard, spectacles, warts, and beauty spots with stray hairs."

I answer with annoyance:

"My dear girl, that chap is a Belgian."

26

"You love me . . . a little . . . Clarissa?"

"That is to say . . . I am annoyed when you leave the receiver unhooked or when you go off to Paris."

"I don't ask anything further."

"Do you love me?"

"No, but you are among women what London is among cities."

"That is?"

"A city which does not wholly satisfy one, but which spoils all the rest for you."

You are jealous. That is, the part of my life which is out of your reach worries you. You cannot tolerate liberty; silence annoys you. You want to know; and knowing isn't enough for you.

You say:

"Describe her."

I answer:

"My mistress has a smooth stomach, firm flesh from which the teethmarks fade quickly, her breasts are set wide apart."

"Young?"

"Very: she pulls corks with her teeth, she sits facing the light, one is not sure to find her at home; she gives herself without nuances, she doesn't want to be loved every day."

"All of which isn't, fundamentally, very amusing."

"For which reason one returns to friends who say: 'I like to please.' 'You're a child.' 'My car can take you.' 'You're uncomfortable, have a cushion.' 'Because I know that you like it . . .'"

Delphine

◄§ I came home in the teeth of a wind whirling stiff as when an express goes through a station. Banking round the wall at the top of Queen's the draught drove its claws to the very bottom of my pockets. My undergraduate gown puffed like a black sail, tugged back my shoulders. I froze, in the March storm, having it a point of honor, like the rest of my fellow students, to go out the year round in low shoes and without hat or overcoat. Many customs had gone by the board since the first school night when a fourteen-year-old French kid had swung his bolster against outraged Anglo-Saxon pajamas in defense of the national nightshirt, muslin with Russian embroidery.

The students who remain in the Dardanelles or at Le Bassée would make a line long as three locks, but even more have returned. The colleges have opened annexes. Oxford is no longer the deserted yard, crossed at certain hours by classless professors, furtive Hindus given to spiritualism, Canadian soldiers doing the town; it is no longer the distinguished cloister of yesteryear but an industrial hamlet to which denizens return from Greek or Latin as from the fields or factories. It is no longer poisoned with elegance and spare time. The education of sons, the heaviest of English taxes, proceeds under restriction. The times of quotidian Clicquot, Clarendon balls, Latin dissertations bought ready-made; the life on credit, when the name of an honorable college would keep the tradesmen from sending you your bills till the end of term your third year. These times have joined those of the earlier

Georges when the undergrads ruined themselves on carriages and kept mistresses. That is why I, like the rest of my fellows, returned to frugal habits, lived according to the rules, dined in hall nearly every evening, even though I lived in the town. We swallowed the dessert, a sort of mocha, alternately yellow and pink, looking like lard and tasting of pepsin, after which we drank water. While the dons said grace the hunks of bread came in on Harris, the old headwaiter who on great days gets out his album of celebrities, Indian viceroys, dukes in gaiters, or even the black velvet cord-edged jacket containing Mr. Oscar Wilde, collector of blue china, who only amazed his time because he stayed a Magdalen man all his life and went to jail instead of paying fines.

I lived in Banbury, a land variegated with cheap villas, wherein there is one Wordsworth House or Keats Lodge for every servant girl you see on the benches receiving kisses on a lipless mouth, despite the bending of spectacles and the breakage of celluloid collars.

I passed, undergraduate, second year, proud of having sworn in Latin, in my dress suit, on the Bible, before the Vice Chancellor; of having fallen into the river, and of getting home from London when possible by the very last train, called that of the fornicators, without falling victim to the University beadles after curfew, master of all I surveyed, because feudal usage allowed me the wall side of the pavement and the middle of the river.

I found in the hall—beneath the deer's horns which supported a gong, by the woodland spectacle of stuffed sea martins—a letter addressed to me. I went up two flights to a room strewn with books, harness, siphons, its walls hung with a toasting fork, the photo of a picture by Dante Gabriel Rossetti, and a cockfight where two men in whiskers and pants strapped under their heels were pushing the birds toward each other with tubes of paper; lit the lamp and read:

> March 13th
> Convent of Saint Marie,
> King Street, Leicester Square,
> W.C. 2.

Dear Jean,

I have been in London for a week. It is ten o'clock in the evening and I have gone to bed without being able to sleep. I have a room in a convent. I hide my eau de cologne, Delphine luxury. They don't permit me to leave my trunk in the corridor. About me there are nothing but pictures of mother; she is still the person who holds the largest place in my life. As my husband is dead, places have no importance. I don't know why I'm not still in Touraine. I took the boat because of a poster. I am a young woman alone. I miss male and female society and yet I don't want it. I am like I used to be in the Loire country, but my nerves are worn out. Now I am sleepy.

Delphine.

*

* *

Delphine.

Things moved over the screen of my window curtains. Landscapes passed over one another, a head appeared on a road, before one could wonder by what trick of forgetfulness shrubbery showed round it, a door, a window, a bourgeois sitting room obliterated a whole tropical landscape and gave way, in its turn, to a cinema booth such as one would see in a cheap park.

My coal-smudged, white-painted wooden mantelpiece disappeared in pink slopes which I recognized as Vouvray, the brass plaque shimmered and spread out into a fluid, sliding and strong, which became in its course the Loire. I thought of a house with two wings joined in a porch, of chintz curtains and a pianola. Delphine exploded with asthma and turned on the overture of *The Barber of Seville,* the long perforated roll flowed down in zigzags, emitting a beady sound. While she played I looked at her hair, the short twisted tufts that I loved. —Life has added nothing to these hours, unless it be that one shouldn't float naturally.— Then I took her hand and thought, "Nothing else matters." The pianola's wind ceased to groan, the notes stopped. I wanted it to stay always like that; but we were serious children; Delphine's aunt, not hearing us laugh, became fussy, and soon two stupid eyes behind the swimming basin of a lorgnette forbade us all tête-à-tête.

They let me play with Delphine who never got her clothes dirty and wouldn't climb the reservoir ladder with me. But her coldness, her intelligence, her "remarks not suitable at her age" displeased my grandparents.

"Delphine," I heard them say, "is the image of her mother." Her mother is living in Toulon with a naval officer. A lady of paleness, with pink fingers, Annamite dresses, never dressed, and who lets the most exotic food get cold without touching it, proud of the days devoted to a table of plausible men, wrinkled and full of maritime disappointments.

Delphine did not live poetically save in her dreams. She told them to me daily and in detail. There was always water, clear when she felt well, often also wild beasts, lynxes, panthers, but very gentle with silky coats. She climbed the trees with them, up to the highest branches, and then fell into the emptiness. She knew the meaning of the dreams "to the bottom," and as this surprised me she confessed that she was in correspondence with Mme de Thebes, and even showed me letters in which the latter "tutoyed" her.

For me, Delphine was a universe. A universe of a more personal inspiration, less anxious about ballots than the one that I lived in.

She said: "I will never be one of the women who accept by saying no."

She went straight on in the full joy of testing words, of practicing ideas. Each experiment was for her an enchantment. No vocabulary seemed unreasonable, no form worthy of discredit. Never letting herself go, she knew nevertheless all the imperfections of the world—limited by the Tours octroi—and although she liked me, she was in no way blinded to mine. She would have liked me to wear spectacles.

I tried to dominate her by intelligence. I lent her *Dominique*. She returned it gravely. "It is beautiful," she said. "You are very sensual," she concluded. It was true. There was a pink flush on my fat cheeks after eating, my nose was attracted by vulgar odors. Delphine seemed to me, on the contrary, measured and personal. So she was, as far as a girl of her age might be, with infinite knowledge, a sure judgment, clever, proud of her ascendancy, at a moment when boys have to live on credit, thanks to hypocrisy or to the indulgence of their elders. Everything lazy, cantankerous, fecund, and untidy in the human race seemed then to have been transmitted into me. I only had to progress. She had only to present life with this firm face, and empty heart, to be at once denounced to destiny, to be bothered and assailed from all sides—as soon as she had risked herself out of doors—by misfortunes, of which her marriage was not the least.

The war was to blame for it all, that's understood. In 1917 there was nothing in Tours to prevent a young French bourgeoise from marrying a Russian officer in soft boots who had followed her for two months; the hospitals were emitting curious vows in all languages, hospital trains were gathered in by respectable ladies who lost control of themselves on smelling gangrene, tea shops were opened round the archepiscopal palace, the edges of the streets were adorned with great umbrellas under which Annamites sheltered young unions.

But this was long after the time when Delphine and I used to bicycle up the bank of the Loire, as far as Luynes, before dinner.

The land was flooded between the cantonal poplars. Evening had come down on the lime cliffs without quenching the sham sunlight of flowering mustard. The river carried a leaded sky; in the meadows the spotted cattle moved slowly, [in] contrabass, after their tongues.

Delphine was peddling against the wind. She wore a cap and a blue woolen sweater. From time to time she moistened her lips, as the wind dried them. Her face rather sulky at rest, or when she was at home, became accessible; reflected in nickel handlebars, she even appeared larger, vulgar, and tonic. At these times I would catch up with her, she would stop peddling and let me push with my hand on the flat of her back.

In sight of Saint-Symphorien the land was no longer wasted. There was room for nothing but vegetables, bistros, and amours. We rested our machines on the slope and went down nearer the water. The sun went down in cloudy insurrection.

With its cloth of generous vain water, its poisonous sky, its lime rock full of caves, Touraine turned savage for a moment. For a moment, also, Delphine was mine; I put my head on her knees, my cheeks scraped by her woolen skirt. My neck swelled, she put her hand inside my collar, maternal, prudent, and excited, saying "You're drenched." Puerile and full of terrestrial passions I kissed her warm hand. Delphine went acid. "I warn you I detest voluptuaries." I didn't insist. I was afraid of the way she made me ashamed, and of the rages my chagrin sent her into.

She seemed to have an extraordinary energy for getting up first. And I followed her.

*

* *

One Sunday about 2 p.m. in the Jermyn Street Turkish Baths, I woke from a short sleep, haunted with nightmares. I had a sore throat, burning eyes, and a stiff solar plexus. I had gone to bed at daybreak after the boat race. Cambridge had won by three lengths—unbearable memory for one year in Oxford. The two teams had started a liquid and fraternal match at the Trocadero banquet that evening, then in howling bunches been borne on taxi tops to a series of music halls, first the Empire, where the stage boxes had kept up an antiphony of yells; then to the Oxford, where the French play permitted improprieties; then the Chelsea Palace, where there was a pitched battle, unpitched by the police; finally on the stroke of midnight London had become an incandescent mass ravaged with pleasures where advertisement-covered buses passed with noise of a rifle range, where the horses bent like our unbendable shirt fronts, portable harmoniums bathed our souls in the water of psalms. The electric sun of the Savoy Theatre was soused out in the Thames, the dubious flowers of clandestine clubs bloomed in the obscurity: Boom-Boom, the Lotus, Hawaii, where the mutilated porter opened a pink curtain on seeing us, displaying behind it a dim face in powdered ocher, a Galician Jew in evening dress with cornelian studs, detaching our tickets from a perforated stub that we might enter the cellar.

I rose, had myself massaged, and went to see Delphine.

At the edge of that nebula of dust and electric gold, whistles, cries, Leicester Square, the French Convent occupies three contiguous pale brick houses and is indicated by the Gothic arch of the chapel door inscribed Dames du Bon Accueil. Next it, the convent door is pierced with a grilled wicket whence blazed the eye of the Sister Doorkeeper, with her hood full of suspicions. I found myself in the parlor, the reception room of a god of the middle class where the water lilies of woven rope mat drowsed on the deep shining floor before the chairs in green rep.

Delphine entered, in mourning, the oval of her face underlined by the white crepe of a bonnet band. I hadn't seen her for five years. We kissed. "Your cheeks aren't as hard as they were," I said, out of cordiality. Her face, smooth as a porcelain bowl, sloped away in an even curve, holding level in its surface her two flat liquid eyes, but my memory hesitated before the softened mouth, weary at its corners and showing no pleasure in possessing its even teeth. The nostrils were open, and lengthened, no longer keeping the delicate line of the nose, tilted, thin to the point of transparency, the only salient in the mask. The expression also had changed, become more taciturn, less often beautified by her old eloquence or assurance. Our joy at meeting was null. "I'm not taking the veil," she said, smiling, "but I need quiet and this convent was recommended me and it suits me. God stretches many snares for us after misfortune, to punish us."

I saw her room, summary as the cheap furnished lodgings of the quarter. The walls were covered with faded crèche paper, blue with gold stars. Lilies of the valley were soaking in the cracked basin. Delphine was dressing for vespers. I consented to go with her.

The guillotine window decapitated a bit of the square streaked with telephone wires which held up an imminent weight of blind sky. The cupolas of the Alhambra, the slipshod Restaurant Cavour, with black Chianti spots on its napkins, cheered this ikon of Sunday with their more Mediterranean elegy.

She took my arm in the street and traces of our old fellowship appeared. "I like being here. The English are queer children, with scurf spots on their hands. They weep over squirrels and sweet peas. They jabber like Southerners, they haven't any lips, are victims of their nerves, and can't in the least or in any way resist their emotions if they ever by any chance happen to have any. They all look like Miss Mabel, my governess at Tours, compliant and distracted both at once. She kept her end up by having a watch with a good miniature on it. At first I thought my husband was in love with her. You never knew my husband? He was like Michel Strogoff in the first act, while he still has his new uniform and all his eyebrows; he was like a tenor I've seen in *Ernani*. That's why I turned round the first time I saw him. He followed us for two months. He wrote me letters on paper alternately red and violet. I was delighted. He asked to marry me. I decided to refuse him myself. Once face to face to him I had

34

panic, and we were married two weeks later. You know how he was killed before Odessa a little later. I haven't forgotten him. He was kind, hot tempered, and crazy, like a Russian. Every time I was in the wrong he wept and begged my pardon, pulling out his revolver. I would have been very happy with him."

Delphine explained what her widowhood had been. Like a long fruitless vigil, in which at midnight she sought signs of hope in herself. "To leave me alone or to keep me company are the two worst services you can render me." Then she had shifted about, through Paris, still uneasy, through various milieux, weeks spent hunting for a "system to live on" or for not disappearing. She found only short reprieves, her time was spent among people without radiance, smeared and rubbed up with intelligence, or atrophied by the hideous habits of pleasure. She refused their mediation.

I refound in Delphine her old impetus, but I divined a diminished resistance and more vehement oscillations under each word. I am no longer much used to young women of my own age having been in France during these last years, only for a short time now and again for examinations. Are they all like Delphine? The older ones always seemed to me abysses of devotion, some attached to their duties, those who preferred pleasure imposing burdens no less heavy upon themselves, all meticulous about obligations, loving life and without revolt against the resistances it offered them. Delphine, on the contrary, does not carry her egoism like a disgrace; she handles it like a curriculum full of intelligence; like a precise, esteemed, and yet exhausting conception. Her dryness of heart is not the same dryness as that of six years ago, but the former doubtless prepared it. She confesses this with such independence that I abstain from passing judgment against her. I divine that instead of finding reasons for enduring, Delphine is ready to destroy herself impatiently; it lends her a tolerable and transient grandeur.

We passed the wax fruits of the Colonial Offices and arrived at Westminster Cathedral, set back from the frenetic traffic which unites Victoria and the Thames. I recognized the sanctuary of the new Catholic faith which had sprouted toward the end of the last century upon the Anglican grass plots. The great Britannic Cardinals Manning and Vaughan willed this witnessing of piety and taste, thanks to which prayer and a modern edifice are not wholly incompatible. One could indeed take pleasure in the bare-brick sincere walls of the basilica, although Delphine pointed with inquietude to a darker line halfway up marking the next layer, the bottom half in too expensive marble and the top half in modern mosaic.

Before the altar hooked by the tongs of pale broken sunlight, a giant Byzantine cross blocked the apse. An obscurity half incense, half outside fog, blunted the domes, their timid window holes. Despite the dressing of chandeliers like Oriental coiffures, superposed iron circles, from which the lamps hung on chains, the cathedral was a monument massive and of public utility like a Roman aqueduct or a railway station. They were saying vespers in the chapel of the Holy Sacrament, the organ erected vast architectural sounds. Across the copper grills the faithful were bathed in composure: two nurses, a City man kneeling before his top hat, a Chelsea Invalid in red uniform, an Indian Army officer in a turban; at the altar three priests officiated. Delphine was silent, her hands over her face. Then she turned a troubled eye toward me, gripping my arm: "Why am I so wicked? Why do I love everything evil?"

Then she smiled at having so exposed her thought to me.

"You are a very small child, I can explain nothing to you."

She led me to the side chapels where one observed the same taste, an art anxious to avoid pomps and archaism. We passed before the chapel of St. Patrick with its veneer of Irish marble, its altar setting encrusted with mother-of-pearl shamrocks. All terrestrial stones, Numidian, Thessalian, and Norwegian, began to stud the church with shopkeepers luxuries. An altar in black marble, like an actress's bathroom, fruit of the offerings of The Great Transatlantic banks, seemed reserved for South American devotions. On the first step a woman was kneeling wrapped in a woolly coat with big folds, half frock and half raglan. I stooped and saw under a hood the face of a made-up flapper, circled [by] frizzed gray hair. The index finger, loaded with a huge cabochon emerald, was ticking off her rosary. I was about to point out this Castilian from the time of the Incas to Delphine when the lady turned and, recognizing my friend, greeted her with three words, jumbled and full of wind, the voice contralto.

Thus I met Pepita Warford, English of Cuban origin, dame

patroness of the Convent now sheltering Delphine. She came toward us, kissed Delphine, spoke to us of the Holy Virgin, of the care of marmosets, and the advantages of night life. Delphine smiled, gushingly, nervously.

Despite my inattention, I couldn't help noticing this singular episode. From the moment I laid eyes on Mrs. Warford, I exhumed in her favor an inconceivable enmity, much less curable than the spontaneous antipathy one feels for anyone called on to play a role in the life of one's friends. It was as if a hypocritical vegetable had suddenly stared at me. Her devotions seemed a culpable industry, and when she fizzed invectives or eulogies in any known language, one thought of a worn-out nightingale.

I was about to dissuade Delphine from the ravages of such acquaintance. I foreboded that they would drag her by sanctified paths toward disturbing renouncements. Then, as Mrs. Warford fell back into prayer, I reflected that no harm ever comes to anyone, and that the abuse of things is a necessary prelude to mastering them. Moreover, a danger is worth its price. I controlled my ill-humor and refused myself any demonstration of cragged wisdom, lest I bring upon myself an outburst of Delphine's wrath, which I hoped soon to see turned, for her own greater good, toward herself.

*
* *

I went back to my University studies. I belonged to no club and played nothing. Spurious champagne, dry cigars and their cost had separated me from the clans where Russian princes, sons of Australians, German Rittersgut set the tone. I was no less alarmed by Baliol strong debaters, the Yankees from St. Johns, and the clerical seed of Worcester and Wadham bursars.

I received letters from Delphine. She displayed a poignant desire for amusement. Written in affliction or in gaiety, they brought me from London a curious savor of indocility, something punctual and premeditated in their outrance which is particularly French, perhaps constituting the politeness of excess. I enjoyed rereading them while at work in the Bodleian, [a] sort of barn where the wooden framework six centuries old strengthens the slightest sound like the soul of a violin, while the shelves, like the planks of a fruit cupboard, align their manuscripts fragrant and drying.

One Sunday evening on my way out to dinner I met Fraser, Professor of All Souls, whose vanity in poetic composition led him to Saturday evenings in Chelsea. He took me to the high table of his College and when the violet-veined Provost, having lined up the cut-glass wine carafes before him at the second course, finally ordered the port to circulate, I learned that Fraser had met Delphine the night before.

"She entered," he said, employing the precious components of the worn vocabulary used in the '8os and no longer current outside University circles, "a public ball in Hammersmith. They have there a unique form of jazz, one hires a partner of either sex for a sixpence. She appeared garbed in black crepe like a parody of a hearse, as if in mourning for her repentance, like Anactoria, bearing the languor of each valse as a new sin on her shoulders, supported by Father W——— [he cited here a Jesuit who had made a reputation by comic sermons] and a curious elderly child, Spanish, clad in a panther skin, whose advantages I could not precisely discern.

"She asked if I knew you, and we spoke of you. After the ball we had early breakfast at her studio. It was all very amusing, but she watched us with a sort of sinister pleasure, her eyes like fire, and her mouth like ashes. Her bruised and precocious heart pleases me.

" 'Heart bruised with loss and eaten through with shame.' One day I will read you what I have written about it."

*

* *

Thus Delphine had, in a few weeks, passed from prie-dieu to noisy Bacchanalia. I was not the least irritated. I couldn't moreover carry prejudice to the point of quarreling with her about it. I didn't then know how many things are possible in London in so short a space of time, which never will be in Paris, the London divisions, the separation of people living side by side, by scorn or by fear of curiosity, being so complete. London is a furtive hermitage, which people find hard to give up once they have sampled it. Only the streets are filled with crowds, cries, advertisements, snobbisms, commercial and sportive prowess; they do not set foot on the gentle deserts where pleasure seems less than elsewhere perishable. Thus I explained to myself that Delphine had made the transit from despair to amusement, which latter seemed to progress toward the worse. I repeated to myself, "What will happen to this friend of your childhood?" without being able to create anything but this factitious bond, external as that of blood relationship. "Why am I so wicked!" I thought again of this question of Delphine's, as the confession of a creature crushed by the consequences only and ignorant of the causes of litigation whose irresponsible stake she was. Her childish despotism, the discipline which she inspired around her, her repulsion from anything that was easy or likely to become a pleasure; ought these to be explained by the fear she had of herself?

"I don't feel well," she wrote. "Since I have stopped amusing myself, I torment myself to fury. I waste my energies to such a point that I will soon have to think of writing nothing but funeral notices. Yet whom shall I say goodbye to? This funereal summer fog, the city warmed like a gridiron, my ignominy, and your disapprobation, which I divine, is it all a bilious attack or what the Abbé Prévost calls English vapors? The sun shines as if through smoked glass, my food tastes of phenol, I can't sleep anymore, and I find only a momentary cool in the parks in the evening, or thanks to the powder (mixed, alas, with too much borax) which I get from a little pharmacy in the Commercial Road."

*

* *

June had come. The students in white flannel devoured a sham summer of icy sunlight and grass ruined by deluge. Doctors in mortarboards went by on the river preceded by a boat bearing trumpets. The families, assembled from the neighborhood, mounted on coaches, offering sugar from one roof to another; the shop clerks in suits such as one saw in last year's revues, endeavored not to catch crabs with their oars, not to bump boats, to show their manners, and call each other "Mister."

The war profiteers took vengeance for a childhood spent in back shops by watching the spectacle of their offspring. They came down from the Narth in nickel-plated cars with a footman's face on each lamp. From some sated province, the actor, Benson, returned with his Shakespearian troop, his poor watery scenery, his shaky moth-eaten fortresses, and we endured, by season ticket, thirty-five acts in one week. The slopes by the roadside were adorned with picnics, iris, broken motorcycles. The countryside became a green desert traversed by short-coated peasants in bowlers. No hollow whitewashed apple tree could avoid bending over water reflecting the clouds, weighted with a boat and the odors of an alcohol lamp. The reeds exhaled the hay fever of phonographs which returned thus to Mother Nature the poesy they had, for their success, borrowed from her. The whole liquid fair continued till the end of term, its assizes accompanied, as at the end of a race, by cries, the noise of rattles, of crackers, of ragtimes, and the odor of bargain tea and stale lemonade, encouraging thus the end of the scholar year.

There was a night fête on Mesopotamia. The college barges lay, each a luminous mass, one half trembling. Corks shot into the river, the rockets coalesced into aqueducts, the Bengal lights spread out a creamy cloth striped by the water. Alone I drove my canoe and its dew-drenched cushions toward the locks. Searchlights disputed even the warm obscurity, catching the ivy-covered church [at] Islington or the singing boats with electric angles. One of these swung into the searchlight as if into a suddenly opened door. I was beside it, but in the shadow, and recognized Delphine quite white, the flare being full in her face, she was smoking. She appeared drunk and gently drifting. Gray crinkly hair emerging from the side of the boat indicated Mrs. Warford's presence in the boat bottom. At the bow, his feet over the water, playing the banjo, sat a dubious individual, apparently Yankee-Italian. He held a lantern in his gorilla jaws, thus illuminating the underside of a C. Chaplin mustache and two sable nostrils. The night again swallowed them suddenly. I saw Delphine throw a lighted cigarette overboard, and it sizzled.

I was confounded and hurt as if the thing somehow wronged me. Not that my own eyes had seen in Delphine this new person whom I had divined, degenerated and a prey of deformed humanity, but that she had concealed her presence from me, here in a place which I regarded as home. Soon after I received a letter in which she said nothing of having left London. I felt deceit in it, then thinking she was perhaps no longer free, I grew anxious. I regretted seeing a creature once perfect given up to these courses, ready to join the sinister cohort of lone women, fed by adventures, the cohort of those whom a deaf but imperious vocation separates from the love of self which saves pretty women, and the natural attachments which satisfy others.

*

* *

It was the displeasure I felt at this incident or the interest in Delphine suddenly, despite the ill-humor it aroused in me, that led me a month later (at the end of the scholar year) to the Ebury Street studio, whose address I had from Fraser.

One reached it through a disused cemetery beneath whose rich lawn the great Anglo-Saxon skeletons, undeformable in death, continued their existence. Outside the garages, men were washing automobiles, thus cooling a street already lightened by its curtains, its brasses, its red doors, its merchants of mirrors and glass "panorama balls," and its makers of [glossy] paper. From the windows of house agents the photos gnawed by the sunlight offered the spectacle of rural bungalows, thickly clad trees, lawns unencumbered.

I had to knock for a long time, although I heard sounds back of the door. Then Delphine's voice, a noise of keys and chains, the door opened on a face pale, puffy with nose accentuated and sharpened. The lids seemed too short for the eyes. I was so struck by it that I couldn't get out my happy small joke about her bolting herself up like an octogenarian.

"Eh, it's you," she said, looking at me with no surprise. Passively she allowed me to enter.

Her expression had changed more than anything else. The eyes were set in a sort of scared stupidity, the glance only moved to shake across mine, refusing to meet it, or lead it to the center of the heart which had been rotted like a fruit. I followed Delphine into the studio, where the livid light completely unveiled this female with gray discolored hair, face going tomato-red, bent back, rolled up in shantung, with slack stockings and slippers. Her back-turned sleeve showed an arm with red, blue, and black spots on it. She forestalled my reproaches. "I've been very ill. I've had abscesses. I was blind for twenty-four hours last week. They are plotting against me."

Delphine looked in the glass, pulled her cheeks, rubbed her forehead.

"I'm like an ecchymosis on the fourth day."

"You always refused to be a victim in the old days."

" 'The old days.' I can't remember them. It's funny. I've completely lost my memory, for some time."

Her phrases faltered. She saw in my eyes that her folly seemed obvious to me. She gathered herself together and tried to select her words.

"It's [a] curious thing," she said, "belonging to a milieu. One doesn't know how it starts, although later it seems as if it had been arranged beforehand by mysterious forces. One is taken somewhere, and one goes back the day after, and the magic circle is closed. One lives in intimacy with people one didn't know and whom one would never have chosen. There is a period when one amuses oneself a lot, the camaraderie, general good humor, an exchange of vital energies make the group a useful personage for whom one neglects little by little, on one pretext or another, everything that doesn't belong to it. Then the rifts begin. The less pleasing element seems naturally to take the chief place. One is bound by repulsions, enmities, not to say foibles. One wants, finally, if not to retire at least to put a little space between oneself and the others. There isn't time. A contact is established, absolute, silent. One can struggle alone, travel, but without getting away; work, amuse oneself, but the group is there watching; in the shape of injunctions, accidents, it finds you again; everything outside it seems inacceptable, save waiting. One communicates only with the initiated, and by odd words which make a language. All of which would be nothing if it weren't that one day, under the influence of dangerous or more hardened elements, which one supposes come from other groups now dispersed, one didn't arrive at a total revision of the content of one's consciousness, at a putting of everything in question, up to the border of chaos."

"Who's brought you to it?"

"As everywhere I've had to do with honest people, and with bad lots, very bad, the former led by the latter. And then, here, it's so funny . . . in Paris there are limits, to everything. In London, there's nothing to hold on to."

"But me," I said, approaching her. "Amn't I here to help you?"

She was no longer listening, was worn out by the effort she had made to think and to express herself.

"Come with me, Delphine. I can't leave you like this. I'm going back to Paris tomorrow. Can I get you your ticket?"

"I couldn't."

"Use your will power."

"Can't."

She sneezed, swollen mucus, red eyelids.

"Let me alone. I don't need your advice or your reproof. I won't stand it from anyone. Besides everything you say is splotched with egoism and ill will. You'd better let me rest as I am. I have fever every day at the same time. Don't inspect those bottles. They don't concern you. Have you come here to spy on me? Don't think you're going to hold an inquest with the servants. There isn't one that will stay."

She listened.

"You hear that gnawing? Those are mice. I'm overrun with them."

She saw that I was incredulous.

"I'm ill, that's it, isn't it? Do you get any pleasure from letting me down, now that I'm a renegade, with dyed hair, dirty nails, slattern. It's a dégringolade, I know that very well. You have observed the process without intervening; from now on I ask you not to bother. Did you use to provoke me to greed? Today I obey a system of misconduct, I'm perfectly comfortable. Your air of superiority annoys me. Go away."

"My dear Delphine, cool off. I am not pitiless, I assure you. Let['s] see if we can't find some way out of it, together."

She weakened, leaned her forehead on my hand, and suffered excessively. Her joints cracked, she crushed her nails into her palms.

I detached myself from her recumbent figure, tried to find, for her, reasons of resistance, or excuses.

"Everything that's happened to me is from pride," she said.

I had awaited this lamentable phrase which every woman has on her lips and by which she defines her humility.

*

* *

Delphine gave me a rendezvous for Regents Park. I first went to register my baggage, for the train for France was starting one hour later. The park about, flayed by five years drilling recruits, was sprouting again. A soldier in peace uniform passed me glowing like a pimento in a bottle of pickles. Dropped by an invisible squirrel a nut fell from branch to branch and broke on the pavement.

I can't say that the visit to Ebury Street the day before had moved me. It had, rather, offended me. Delphine suffered, without contentment, attached to her adversity, prey to a disconcerting vulgarity. Then she had talked like a feuilleton, and a fainting fit had finished the general wreck of things. But as soon as I was alone the rigorous resolute image of yesterday returned to me, and as if glued upon this by decalcomania, her recent disorder grimaced at moments. It pained me. Not that Delphine's happiness was precious to me, but it worried me to see this thing bend, this nature of which neither pleasure nor misfortune had been able up till then to destroy the unity. I had thought her incapable of amendment, but also unliable to contagion. Her proud integrity had often been unsupportable, but this brutal capture of all of her by an utterly useless destiny was none the less so.

I then felt an affectionate commotion, and thought only of devoting myself to . . . All the night I was consumed with inquietude. I sought ardently the happiness of saving her. Overwhelmed with tenderness I almost got up, to go to awaken her. . . .

The hour passed. Delphine did not arrive. London never gives back anything given up to it. Like an open net it receives and keeps everything. There are in these rows of houses many like her, not kept there by any precise grief or pleasure, and yet who cannot leave. Without crushing them between its stiff quays, London takes the products of the world into its marine esophagus, swallows them, and they stay there where the boat stops.

She wouldn't come. In the zoological garden, the reinforced concrete caverns shook with the howls of the menagerie, the erythrocyanus or large red-and-blue macaw lacerated the evening air with its cries. I remained alone with my heart full of charities.

Aurora

◆§ Morning had not yet plumbed the courtyard beneath the open window; above me was the worn sheet-iron sky, bolt-studded with stars, and already acid-stained toward the Orient. A good day for a hanging. The courtyard was a cry for air receiving no echo. It was too narrow for a flat silence; and contained therefore a vertical one, such as you could have put in a drainpipe.

In their cellarage the bakers' assistants were flopping down their huge lumps of dough, as if each thud were the last.

I don't want to live here any longer, I choke; sleep might be possible but for one's dreaming and the crushing fatigue of waking; it is more impossible to live away from one's friends than with them. I bite my nails, scratch my body hairs, invent receipts which, failing to kill time, leave it disabled.

I should like to go off alone, with my checkbook slung round my neck in a reasonable small iron case; and a valise. My valise with cheeklike sides, tanned by all the winds, stroked by all fingers, labeled by hotels and station officials, chalked, piebald by customs houses, the lining blue-sweated by sea water and sea sickness, and reddened by breakages of cologne bottles. Unfortunately I can no more escape from this city than I can escape from myself. There remain the walk round the yard, the domesticated herbage of Upper Tooting, suburban motorbuses, parks as inept as a flowerpot on a balcony, and, under the colonnade back of the opera, the odor of agricultural labor, investing the art of Thomas Beecham with the fragrance of cabbages.

I hear people amusing themselves behind me. Is there one among them who would leave his diversions and follow the indications which seem to be imposed by my reading of the morning? who would live with me? or at least join me in a regret at not leaving? or console me for the anonymous farce of creation? Or perhaps one could advertise in the papers?

I turn round: a woman in an orange tunic tied with a gold cord, her bare arms are sunburnt and very long. There is tattooing round her wrists. It is Aurora. I recognize her as having danced under the rain in the open air theater at Bagatelle one summer evening. There are also the illustrated covers of the *Tatler*: "Aurora feeding her pumas." "We walk badly. How Aurora sets down her foot." A black diamond, alas from the Burlington Arcade, ornaments her first finger.

Despite which she is pleasing. She speaks simply, as if used to economizing her breath, her words are numbered. In the center of a circle of young men, she is of similar shape, narrow hips, short hair, small head, her eyes meet theirs on a level.

She says:

"Women, odalisques. Too short in the leg, when they challenge a man their eyes are on a level with his lips, he looks into their corsage; is it serious?"

Aurora has no corsage and deprives us of furtive pleasures only.

This evening there are society women. Before them Aurora loses all her assurance, she does not like them to look at her, she hides her gilded sandals and bare toes under her tunic, she moves her brooch higher, reducing the aperture of her décolleté.

All the other women, on the contrary, go to her with their confidences, kiss her hands, put their pretty cosmetic'd bonbonlike faces on her shoulder, and tell her tempestuous tales figuring generals, producers, servants, suicides, purveyors, and "coco" merchants. During which Roger, with heaving flanks, wrings *Parsifal* from the piano.

I am sleepy. Fatigued to the point where it rests one to say one is tired and to do nothing further about it. The conversation is pasty. I go to the feeding room. The plates still offer a few dried sandwiches turned up at the corners like ill-stuck postage stamps; cigarette ashes, corks; the liquid level is low in the bottles; the guests' beards increase implacably. One's hands are sticky, and one's face is uncomfortable.

I return to my window. The street is now blue, cold, and steely. Under some "S"-shaped roof tiles a woman works a sewing machine, trying to stop the night's raveling with her hem. I feel a pointed chin going into my shoulder. I feel a breast dilate against my back, inhaling the air of the new day which the park leaves have at last washed and sent back reflavored.

"What a life!" said Aurora.

I replied:

"What a life!" but did not pay much attention to what I was saying. I had no longer the energy to remember who we were or why we were there or whether Aurora pleased me or displeased me, neither had I the inclination to modulate my voice or my welcome, or be charming, or open my eyes.

Aurora said: "Whose house are we in?"

"I don't know. I came with friends . . . Champagne warm and too sweet . . . let's go . . . where's the door?"

"Ah!" said Aurora with impetus, "to live simply and logically, in harmony with oneself and the world, the equilibrium of the Greeks, the joy . . ."

I came to myself at the sound of these imbecilities, finding in my nerves an energy my muscles denied me, exasperation awoke me. I felt like asking her why she came out dressed like a guy, why she camped out like a Tzigane instead of living under a roof like everyone else; I wanted to stamp on her perfect gilt-sandaled feet, and wring her neck afterward. I thought of exercises in fairs under police supervision, of the poor saltimbanques in the rain, I spewed from me the Helvetian heresies and visions of art. Nothing would calm me except disparaging and humiliating her.

"Say, can you do a split?"

"Sure."

She arranged two chairs and began to bisect herself. It was too much. I leapt at her to strangle her. I exerted all my strength on her powerful neck, but she smilingly stiffened her muscles from chin to shoulder, and I finally had to let go, exhausted.

She laughed. I was furious.

"Come," I said, "I'll see you home."

Aurora ascends into a taxi as if into a chariot. The conveyance moved silently. Aurora sat in the shadow, her legs crossed, her chin in her hand.

Calmed, I temper my thoughts with benevolence:

"She has really simplified herself, extraordinarily. No deceit passes her thin lips, and no emphasis, no trouble drips from her eyes, her hands make no useless movement. She orders her body about as lucidly as she would an instrument of precision, with powerful delicate wheels, against which the fatigues that demolish the rest of us beat in vain. Even at this hour her organs function correctly."

I envied her her harmonious perfection, her inner life without conflicts, her joints without arthritis, her cornless feet, and the unstiffenable small of her back.

If I should ask:

"What keeps you from sin when you feel like it, [since] you're sure of not having a headache the day after?"

She would answer:

"My hygiene."

Suddenly Aurora burst out: "Don't leave me alone! not alone!" Sobs.

They twist the hard-muscled body, and shake it convulsively. I try to take her hands, their tendons stand out like steel wires, but the hands are clamped over her eyes, over her forehead, bulging and hard as an armor plate. Warm tears fall on my hands, which I try to use gently, but the gentleness is no use. I leave Aurora to herself.

She weeps.

She is trying to live simply. That's all.

Aurora is domiciled near the river. First there are vacant lots, then a street of workman's houses, a Gramophone snores behind a red blind. There is an iron grill, a flagstone walk between orchards. Curious landscape in the small hours.

Aurora scratches a match. I am in a room with trunks, packing cases marked THIS END UP. BOTTOM. P. & O. CABIN. Books, piled on the floor. On a low bed, without bedclothes, lie some sable furs and a broom.

Thence we enter the studio. The obscurity is punctured by four luminous dots: Aurora turns on four blue-bodied gas butterflies. With the first two the walls approach, consolidate their masses, and reveal the form of the room.

With the two others, the darkness is detached from the corners, mounts to the ceiling, and disappears. The twenty-foot walls show arches in relief, supporting the windows.

Aurora pokes up the stove. The glow spreads over the floor and reaches a distant mirror. The room is bare. Here and there casts from the antique rear waxy patina from their pedestals. At the back of the room, a platform.

It is the trial room of a law court abandoned in the time of George IV. Over the doors the inscriptions: ENTRANCE FOR THE PUBLIC. THE DEFENDANT. THE ADVOCATE FOR THE CROWN. THE ATTORNEY GENERAL. Under the judge's bench is Apollo autochthonous, at his feet a piano (mechanical). There is no other furniture but two sofas, the jury box, some African taborets, some Zambezi hangings with geometric designs.

"This is my house," said Aurora. "It's really a trunk. I own nothing in the world but these casts, my dresses, and my guns. I used to have a big house in Portman Square, with furniture, and people, and servants to pass things round on trays. I haven't the sense of possession, I haven't kept anything. I am poor. I have gradually freed myself from the tyranny of things, the chains laid on us by things we love because of their beauty or price or memory."

"And now?"

"Now I am left alone in life, sitting on my boxes, face to face with myself."

"You are as beautiful as another man's wife, Aurora. Is it true that you belong to nobody?"

"No one ought to enter my life."

"You are in love with your body."

"It's a deposit that's been confided to me. I don't put dirty thoughts or dirty food into it, I look after it, I respect it, I clothe it simply . . . I am thirsty."

She lifted a bottle of Australian burgundy from a place on the floor, next the wall. Chambertin—Big Tree Brand. She took a swig from the bottle.

Aurora annoyed me.

"You ought to be a reformer, a vegetarian, a rhythmic gymnast, a teetotaler. I hate this defiance of morals, this puritano-pagan regeneration of society."

"You are wrong. I'm not doctrinaire in the least. I'm a Canadian, fond of rough life."

"Since when?"

"Since always. I can't remember when I danced, or held a rifle for the first time . . . but tonight for the first time, I feel tired. Gina dragged me on after the theater to that place where I met you. I'm sorry. I'm very tired. I look at the road before me, like a bad runner, and I hesitate. Public performances use up my vitality. You saw how I was in the taxi . . . I'm feeble, nervous . . . and to have you looking on . . . it's very odd."

Morning sleep will refresh her; but she begs me not to leave her alone; asks me to come upstairs while she bathes.

I was apprenticed to the simple life.

Above the door to the back stairs one reads: WARDROBE OF THE LORD JUSTICE. We entered thereby the bathroom.

She cried out:

"Get in Aurora."

She disrobed herself in the simplest possible fashion, entered the water, soaped herself, splashed water over herself. Perfect body. The back muscles moved like ivory balls under the sunburnt skin, stretched, a tissue solid and precious as silk for airships; one could pick out the muscles as easily as on an anatomic chart, where their rubicund arborescence is shown covering our organs; the bent flanks are flush with the water, the prowlike breasts, the long legs stripped of all overweight by her dancing, slender at the ankles, hollow inside the thigh, filled amply over the knees.

"Get out, Aurora!"

She talks to herself, to her clothes, to things. ("A habit of all solitaries," she explains. "When they pass months without seeing anyone, they need the sound of the human voice, as a tuning fork for the other senses.")

She thumps herself, rubbing her face till it was blood red, without fuss. No powder, no rouge, no perfume.

"What are you laughing at?"

"For the first time," I said, "I am laughing at the thought of a corset, of a collar, and buttoned boots."

There is a good odor in the room, washed flesh, soap, alcohol, steam. Aurora opens a cupboard where ribbons and scarfs are laid in a prismatic row; she puts on a crêpe de Chine veil and goes down to the studio.

The gas butterflies return to their cocoons. Aurora rolls herself in woolen blankets, and stretches out on a mattress, chucked there onto the floor. She then makes sure that her revolver is under the bolster. Her naked arms and shoulders project from the improvised bed. One sees her straight nose in the midst of her bushy hair. One sees her eyes. And then does not.

I leave the studio, and go to a cabman's shelter for coffee.

I returned to Aurora's.

After work I sought the river where the draft from the North Sea breaks westward through the smoke, beating down the sea gulls and the smell of the exposed city mudbanks. The streets leading thither were hardly marked out, full of puddles; one already smelt the fields and felt the country was near one.

"You ought to come out of town with me," said Aurora. "I would teach you to live like us savages. We could go swimming in no more time than it takes to dine in a restaurant, or we could take to the woods. On summer nights I'll take you to sleep out on Oliver's Terrace, you can see the Crystal Palace shining like a carbuncle under the moon. You'd feel better, you'd have no more headaches, your hair'd stop coming out; you'd lose your French habit of wanting your friends' mistresses."

The taxi stopped in the middle of the road as if for a breakdown. But the chauffeur neither swore nor lifted his cap. He opened the door. I'm there. I had promised to be at Epping Forest at seven. I am.

It is a September evening, somewhat cool. The great beeches repose on the resilient soil, neither their shadows nor human labor seem to weigh down the earth. (If you can say that English farm labor ever does weigh.) The Gramophones cease wailing from the river. The deer move through the early mist.

Aurora had promised to be here at seven. Doubtless she reckons the time by the sun, she will excuse herself, her lateness on account of the mist as others would on account of a block in the traffic.

Suddenly the branches crackle under a weight that has scarcely touched them; a doe's? I turn; here is Aurora. She runs toward me, her tunic glued against her like the Victory's. She carries an attaché case. She runs on her toes, with even strides, well-balanced from the hip. She slows up thirty yards from me. Her face, which had been merely a bright disk, becomes definite, divided horizontally by her high cheekbones, relieved by a short nose mobile as a police dog's. Her onrush moderates itself gradually, she reaches me at a walk. She puts down the attaché case, places her two hands on my arms.

"You have done well to come."

"How long have you been here, Aurora?"

"Since last night. I slept under the stars. Gina brought me out and left me here after the theater. I went up to the hollow oak and stretched out on the grass, I have had apples to eat, I've looked at London through the branches. This morning I went down to the village, it was from there that I telephoned."

"You'll be jugged for that costume, Aurora."

"The forest guard's a friend of mine. I think you'll undress too!"

I refused. She took my hand and led me to a shack covered with dried oak branches, knelt before me and lighted the fire; balanced a frying pan on two stones and offered me eggs and bacon. I had some difficulty in getting used to her thus, her knees black with earth, her hands greasy, her ensemble dirty and natural, I mean, returned as it were to nature; the upturned tunic revealed her thighs, suave, rosy, and muscular in the sunlight, and also the details which long heredity had made so secret and so desirable to me.

I had to give way to Aurora, removing my socks and collar.

Then catching her expression, I relinquished my braces, and stood, in my turn, naked, a red streak where my collar had been, a blue band where my garters had been, blinded by the acrid smoke of green leaves, like a general stripped naked by Tuaregs, but still bearing an oak-leaf insignia on his kepi.

Wood pigeons streaked the sky. Aurora took my cane, aimed at them, and fired both barrels, but the birds continued in their course, anxious to reach the Nelson column before nightfall.

"I was born in Canada," said Aurora, "by the lakes. Fly fishing for salmon, colored flies, two men put a pole through the gills to carry the big fish. The women give themselves without fuss, lie on the beds of white heather. I finished with all that very young. Both my parents were dead. They came from Westmoreland. My mother was very beautiful. I hardly knew her. She had the smallest foot in the world—couldn't get my big toe into one of her slippers. She had black hair and the complexion of a keepsake heroine. 'Like waves on a lake came her hair / To die on the strand of her brow,' as Wordsworth says. When she went up to London for the season, she broke everyone's heart. But she loved my father. She followed him to Canada when he decided to live there. She spent most of her life lying down and died young.

"I get my wild tastes from my father. He let me climb trees and cliffs, up to get gull's eggs, and down them to get seashells. I always went hunting with him. I rode as soon as I could walk. I followed him like a dog. That's what I had, a real hunting dog's education. I learned to judge a town by its smell, people by their tracks, to stay downwind, to collect game in the worst places, and in winter, I waded into pools in up to my waist to get the ducks he shot down. I can still see him waiting for me on the bank in his checked breeches, and velvet cap, with his duck gun, and smiling in his white beard."

I was cold, but I wanted to stay there for the evening. I had stripped off the townsman, the simple life appeared good and beautiful; I gave up my room in Mayfair, the steaming bath then ready, the clean starched shirt, waiting, spread out on my bed. I gave up the advantages of a coat padded over the shoulders, smooth hair, and conversational wit. All I needed to do was to sign an agreement at the end of the month, to retire, I have no more needs, I no longer expect anything from anybody, social revolutions need not alarm me, I scorn the workingman who needs cinemas and apéritifs. I own nothing but the two hundred and eight segments of my skeleton. I'm at the earth-level, I am the first to profit by the magnetic solar currents, I am the burner, the first consumer of the air's oxygen. I am going to owe it all to Aurora, to be healthy, to think sanely and to live according to the law of the earth.

"Good night, baby, God keep thee," she said.

She left me thus for the night journey as for a dangerous enterprise from which we might not return. Already I heard the trumpets. The pure air was an anaesthetic, for the first time in my life I was about to sleep out of doors.

I caught an angina under the stars. Aurora made me tisanes by the fire in her studio. Then she narrated:

"I got to India in 1909, from Aden. We were going twelve knots an hour over a tin-plated sea on an autumn morning. I saw the brick front of Bombay. The sky was stretched over the factory chimneys like a silk canopy, to the right and left up to the Elephanta cliffs. The wake of the smoke lay in the sky longer than the screw's wake on the water.

"I stayed six weeks on the peninsula. I wanted solitude, I wanted to run in dry air, I wasn't satisfied to stay in low countries. The rivers were like corrosive swamps, and the ports atrociously depressing. I hate stuffy valleys where they hunt only small game. I made up my mind to go to Kashmir and Tibet. I went from Srinagar up to the mountain lakes in the pine wood. The higher we went, the colder it was. The natives slept on the march. I had to wake them with a whip. We cut steps in the ice, always going higher and . . ."

Aurora pointed to studio windows where night was about to descend for certain all too abbreviated hours. Then her hand returned to mine. Why did she need my hand in hers, which cuts steps in ice, and can bend a penny like a stick of marshmallow? Her feet have known only sandals. They have trod the burning snows, the red sands of Somaliland, and scattered the subterranean palaces of the Gabon ants who pass their nights sawing hard earth.

Frost, salt, rain, mud, sweat, deluges, perfumes have passed over her body. Iron, lead, and stone have all wounded it. I hold her bullet head in my hands, it is hard as a paving stone, the thick hair does not deaden the contact. An incomparable caress on the bushy short shock, clipped down by scissors and shaved off abruptly at the nape. I put my fingers on her granite forehead, on her cheekbones that stick out like small cobbles. While she talks I amuse myself by moving her arms and legs. The muscles rise and fall silently.

Aurora is covered with scars. I have pointed to these seriatim, and she explains them. A Rhodesian buffalo stepped on her; in a dangerous double jump in Carolina she was thrown off her horse and they thought she was dead. This hole in her occiput? She fell through a trapdoor at Olympia.

So many accidents and so few adventures. So many shipwrecks, such a love of boats, departures, her whole life spent as if life were only movement. No habits: only a few cooking receipts and some notions of hygiene. Courage used for dining without meat, and sleeping in unheated rooms. So much kindness, silent and practical kindness; elementary instruction which no one had ever given me, and which you can't find written down anywhere. An organic gaiety, always equal, taken out of the air's oxygen and passed on to her surroundings, one of these gaieties that are more attractive than vice, snobbism, or love. A soul scoured like her body, cleaned like a gunbarrel; helping hands, generous heart, a transmuter of energy, machinery for the transmission of power, pleasant fruit of the earth, the product of my hunt, valuable animal momentarily captured, Aurora . . .

Aurora has rented a loft in Dulwich for her saddles, rods, hunting kits, and utensils. She has some stuffed heads at a taxidermist's in Covent Garden. But her real treasure—her guns are at Kent's.

They are shapeless objects wrapped up in old rags, first aid to steel damaged by oxides. But when Aurora unwinds the wrappings, the barrels appear shiny and ready. Aurora balances a Holland & Holland .16 caliber over her first finger, the balance is perfect. The barrel blue. She turns the loosened screws with her thumbnail. The weapon is designed in a double curve, a round cross over the grip, from which the barrel spreads in its straightness. The magazine hangs under its belly holding the spare cartridges as if they were eggs.

"Here's my favorite. Wollaston .10 caliber, for big game," said Aurora. "It came from Major ———'s sale. It's a comrade, a good comrade this gun. We can kill a hippo as easy as killin' a rabbit."

And she runs her hand over the hammerless from rearsight to grip.

Hippopotami, huge double-boiler bellies, wallowing in delta mud, crocodiles with little round tummies, damp like a lettuce, with hamadryads sitting on their cheeks, brown bears, their paw pads more delicious than honey, hyenas like bags of bones, all dead by Aurora's hand, finished off by this .10 caliber, am I going to love her?

No. It turned out otherwise.

This evening, the last, had however begun very well. Aurora and I had dined at old Shepherd's in Glasshouse Street, where I like the heavy tables, low ceiling, the toasting forks, and the cold buffet with jonquils in ginger-ale bottles. One is shut off by the cubicles, over which appear the wrinkled baldness of Sargent or the tufts of Roger Fry's fleece.

Aurora was explaining how you hunt in Abyssinia, in East Africa, in Nigeria. Notable hunters had allowed her their company. They were simple folk, strong, silent men, trappers, solitaries, hunting "cleanly, roughly, without fear, the great race that sweated in Africa" when ivory was a trade, and before it was the stake in a game. They took their lives in their hands, nothing between them and extinction but an old gun that took more than a minute to load, man against beast, men who ate what they shot, and who when they shot nothing, ate nothing.

Aurora despised the rich modern young man who goes out from Mombasa with sixty bearers for an easy and healthy hunting ground.

Aurora's stories made me sleepy. It was after nine. The restaurant, like a frigate of Nelson's day, had put up its porthole-like shutters. We consumed Welsh rarebit and port.

I was arriving with her in inaccessible unhealthy countries, where one has to leave things behind, first the useless objects, then the bearers struck down suddenly with mysterious illness, then the friends killed by luminous flies . . .

And I thought:

Will Aurora leave me, likewise, one day in the antipodes, and come back alone, after extraordinary years, or will she leave me tomorrow on a bench? All things are possible. I really don't care very much for the extremities of adventure.

Another fruity port.

No. Aurora will not exercise this influence over me. She amuses me, that is all. She will pass, I will remain quite alone, drowsing under my old yellow Buddhistic fat . . .

We go out. Aurora suggests the Café Royal. It is time for absinthe, taken there, ritually, after dinner. A humanity materializes little by little under the acrid smoke of Birman cheroots, under the gilt ceiling, shut in by the red plush, and the mirrors showing their multitudinous columns. Artists in khaki, Polish in outline, playing dominoes with their mistresses or their sisters. Later one will meet sour Y.W.C.A. females whom one had seen at shows of wood engravings. Musicians of the mobilizable school preparing distant tours for propaganda, Jewish special constables, with armbands, with their eyeglasses chained over their projecting ears, are waiting until it is time to man the searchlights.

Art gives only a conditional support to the war. The Royal Academy paints the General Staff with fervor, the Independents freighted with conscientious objection dedicate themselves to the motor trucks.

Daniel comes up to our table.

"Montjoye's giving a supper this evening. He wants me to say that he has tried in vain to get you on the telephone, and that he wants you to bring Aurora, whom he is very anxious to know."

Montjoye, or rather Aronsohn (Daniel says it's an old Norman family), is a private secretary to the Chancellor of the Exchequer. He has an Adam apartment in the Albany, ornamented with "natures mortes" (the deaths having been violent). They are tinted blue, there are black satin armchairs painted by Conder, and Coromandel trunks, the patterns sawed down to the thickness of leaves. He don't mind standing drinks after the theater.

"I won't go to Montjoye's," said Aurora. "He's unhealthy. He exhales an odor of corruption."

"You talk like the Archbishop of Westminster."

"He's been asking me for a long time. I wouldn't ever go. You can put it down to my uncouthness . . ."

I shrug my shoulders.

Incomprehensible people are very annoying. I know that Aurora *will* go to Montjoye's, she always goes anywhere she's invited. Just as she stays in town and goes on about the forests, as she goes to the Carlton proclaiming that she likes to cook her food between two stones, as she goes naked from snobbism or from bashfulness; as she claims to have brought order into her life, which is one long incoherence, ineptitude, and confusion. What use are her disciplines, leading only to the absurd and ephemeral existence of women such as one meets on steamers, in hotel lobbies, at charity performances, and who have at least the merit of naiveté, or vice, or stupidity?

I know, having often been there, that Montjoye's evenings aren't made for Aurora, or for any woman one cares about. But she's got to go there in order to see for herself that there are nothing but buffaloes and mugs.

"I've got a taxi," said Fred, "and I'll drop you."

Montjoye opens the door himself. His mass detaches itself from the yellow hangings of his hallway. He opens the door with a blend of curiosity and terror, as if he expected you to smack him for the interest he takes in your affairs. When he manages to get into my rooms his phrase of greeting is, "I'm going in just a moment." Then he stands on the threshold until one says, "Anyhow shut the door." After which he risks bashfully, "In front of me or behind me?" He looks only at Aurora, pays no attention to Fred and myself, greets her familiarly:

"Aurora, here and at last!"

He takes both her hands and fondles them, leads her under the lamp with black pendants, takes off her cloak with his own especial and inimitable gall.

"How beautiful you are."

Supper is served for eight in his circular salon. Grünfeld, the officious Bolshevik agent, the Duchess of Inverness, a Dutchman named Bismark, Gina, and a few actors.

Montjoye takes Aurora's arm, smiles at her embarrassment, pours out her drink, places her next the Duchess. I loathe Montjoye. My thought returns to him when I try to remember when I began to spew at people of taste. I cannot describe the irritating finickiness of his apartment. From the disks of the doorknobs, the candelabra with green candles, from the monogrammed cut-glass tumblers, everything is perfect. In a corner of the room on a table that has been pushed back to make room for dancing, there are a pile of dossiers: *Credits to the Allies, Advances to the Bank of France, Extraordinary Expenses.* The whole work of the Ministry is there, in disorder amid tuberoses and photographs. And with his genius for figures Montjoye can get it all fixed up for his chief by morning, instantaneous labor, if there are to be questions in the House, or a Conference.

"One can't get you drunk, Aurora, but promise me to drink this, I have made it specially for you."

He feverishly shakes a bottle containing four layers of liqueur, and approaches the fire, which lights up his grotesque face, fat head, and gray hair.

Fred seats himself at the piano. Grünfeld having found a Pushkin in the library, declaims.

"Don't believe it!" says Montjoye. "He don't know a word of Russian."

The immobile Duchess descends on us each in turn, through her lorgnette with a frigid eye. She has the sterile youth of fifty-year-old American females, exquisite feet, white hair and jade teeth. She is in nurse's uniform with a great cross of rubies on her forehead.

Aurora is somberly absent-minded. She accompanies Fred at the piano. I try to get near her, and to join in singing,

"All dressed up and nowhere to go"

which Hitchcock, half asleep in his chair, having made it swears that he can't remember. On a divan in the corner Montjoye talks to the Duchess in an undertone with suppressed gurgles.

"Aurora is going to dance," he says, getting up suddenly and leading her to the center of the room: "Wait, Aurora, I'm going to make you a carpet, a carpet of flowers, a carpet of pearls, a carpet for your beauty, for your grace . . ."

He hesitates, no longer knowing what he is saying, he empties the vases, and throws the flowers on the floor.

Everything goes round. Everything still whirls round in my memory, Grünfeld's red beard, Montjoye's pasty countenance, and Aurora, especially Aurora, unclothed, between four lotus-shaped lanterns, her arms stretched out, gleaming with sweat, as if possessed, leaping wildly from one corner of the room to another, turning on her own axis, whirling with mechanical swiftness, leaving on our retinas an image like a Hindu god's, the multiple legs and arms. She falls to the floor, Montjoye kneels near her, wiping her forehead with his handkerchief. He leans over her to inhale her, closes his eyes. I see the mesial vein stand out on his forehead, the neck swells behind his collar. His head approaches nearer and nearer, then draws back; then losing all control of himself he places his lips on Aurora. Aurora shivers, opens her eyes, comes up with prize-fighting speed, lands right on the jaw, knocking Montjoye into the fender. Montjoye howls horribly. A bottle of crème de menthe spreads its emerald contents over the floor.

"Aurora has started a pogrom," says Fred, impassively, from the piano.

I try to intervene.

"Let me alone," said Aurora, "I hate you."

And before anyone can move, she has jumped out of the window into the ground-floor garden and disappeared.

When I entered the studio Aurora was seated on the bed, her chin in her hands, her elbows on her joined knees. She did not turn her head toward me, I advanced, meeting her eyes, but her glance went through me, to the wall immovably.

I put my hands on her shoulders: she trembles.

"Let me alone. Leave me. I never want to see you again. Go!"

I sit.

"Go."

I get up.

She softens and holds out her hand.

"Sit down. I only wanted to say that you'd better leave me alone from now on. You're no use to me. I don't want to say anything more."

She pokes the point of her umbrella through the lacing of her sandals.

"I was beginning to reap the fruits of my wilful labor. I'm not a nun. I ought to invent the rule and keep it. The renouncement isn't easy for a wild creature like me. As you haven't watched the whole long struggle, you simply can't understand . . . Evenings like last night don't straighten things out . . ."

Tears stream down her cheeks. I wanted to say . . . but she interrupted me, rose, and covered herself with a violet veil.

Great zinc clouds break into the sunset. It thunders. Taxis rush by, quite mad.

As soon as we are out of her quarter people begin to look round. Aurora stops. There is the thickness of the veil between us, very dry.

Aurora trembles.

"You will pardon me, Aurora?"

Vague gesture on her part, which I interpret as:

"It isn't your fault."

She makes a sign. Number 19 bus comes docilely to curb at her feet. She ascends the stair like a frieze unrolling itself.

The signboard says she can stay there till she gets to Islington.

I am sorrowful. I know that I shall never be unhappy, not really, except after dinner.

❧OPEN ALL NIGHT❧

Catalan Night

꒰ I was going to travel with a lady. Half of her already adorned the compartment; the other half, thrust through the compartment door, still belonged to Lausanne station and to a delegation of men of divers nationalities, merging into one shadow on the platform and wearing each an eglantine in his buttonhole. Bells jangled. Travelers glided over the asphalt. The scarlet fruit of the signal fell from its latticed trunk in obedience to the timetable. The noise of the whistle pierced the compartment. The lady shook hands over the lowered window: a freckled Britannic hand, a fat German one, the parchment hand of a Russian, some slender Japanese fingers. Finally a young Spaniard, with a boil hidden beneath his hunting-stock, offered a dirty copper-ringed paw, saying:

"Adios, Doña Remedios!"

The crowd opened, a mauve star moved through the breach dragging in its wake a muffled noise and a smoke trail through which the film turned without further waiting, dutiful and distrait.

One by one the train broke the handclasps, its hawsers, and slid onward, thus lightened.

I heard a shout: "Vive l'Internationale!" devoured on the instant by the turning disks and the velvet of a tunnel. The lady remained imprudently thrust through the aperture, waving. I dissuaded her, putting my hand on her dimpled shoulder and pointing to the enameled notice:

IT IS DANGEROUS TO ALLOW CHILDREN TO LEAN
OUT OF WINDOWS

at this she smiled and turned toward me.

Lovely, lovely, pretty, unusual. Fortune was compensating all at once for the deceptions of so many other departures, when the lady with whom one wanted to travel had remained on the platform and the accompanying male taken the place beside one, without one's having been able at all to distinguish, up to the ultimate instant, which was leaving; so had they seemed equally moved, equally full of excitement, clad in tweeds equally fancy.

The emergence from the tunnel spoiled nothing. From behind a somnolence which I pretended was submerging me, I read my companion's features, like a map, in order not to take the wrong turning. A captivating country, full of surprises, bounded by shoes and her hat. One envied passport officials who can designate daily so many faces, cold, warm, different as the petals of fingerprints.

In this one everything was sincerely rounded and moderate: the dimpled cheeks, the heavy mouth, the forehead, the high cheekbones, which seen in three quarters prevented one's glance reaching the pupils, cutting the latter as it were on the bias, quite irresistibly, and preparing one of those stage entrées labeled "from the wings," which deceive no one and yet manage to charm. The bosom rose in a gentle slope toward a thick throat ornamented formally with false pearls and overshadowed by a young, heavy chin. On her first finger shone a sapphire circled with brilliants; between short thighs her foulard dress sank in a hollow. Her mittened hands were clasped flat over her knees; her feet were arched until they seemed swollen and did not reach to the floor; her hair, on her removing her hat, appeared absolutely stretched to the ears and there permitted to escape, foamy and almost agile, and so oily that it ceased to be black and gathered all colors in its refraction; the chignon twisted like a towel and dripping with rhinestones; in all of it Spain was apparent.

She leaned her head against the knitted railway embroidery and slept without effort. Perhaps I had hypnotic powers?

When we reached Morges a storm broke suddenly. Thunder

burst over the peaks, drowning the noise of the train. There were groans. My companion woke with a start and made the sign of the cross without knowing it. Surprised, she looked as do other Southern women when they travel, like a bird with its feathers ruffled; the youngest change and harden, the others go a lead gray and subside behind the shine of their jewelry. The sky ripped like a piece of silk. Lightning had just struck the ballast, quicker than the magnesium of a reporter's flashlight. I offered to lower the curtain.

"I am not afraid of the storm, but my little dog, here, in the basket, doesn't like it."

Then as if the thunder had in some way denuded her, she opened a bag and reconstructed her face behind a dustcloud of rice powder. A white lock appeared in her hair like a steam jet amid coal smoke. The groans began again under the seat and continued until she made up her mind to remove a base-born fox-terrier with long fawn-colored ears from the gilded basket inscribed: "Souvenir of the Righi." I opened my suitcase, displaying a bear and a red donkey. She congratulated me on my menagerie. For my part, I paid compliments to her dog such as are only allowable in suburban locals.

"Trick is ugly, Monsieur, but I love her. She's all I have left in the world."

"Your send-off at Lausanne didn't look it. Of course, I'd just got to Lausanne a few hours before. I don't know what you have done to deserve so much limelight. You've been giving a charity performance at the Casino?"

"No, Monsieur, I am not wholly an actress" (she held the tip of her tongue between her teeth for a moment when she pronounced the last part of the word—the teeth small as rice grains)—she placed a weary smile at my service—"although I have played a role in the most horrible judiciary parody of the century. My name is Remedios Sirvent, and I was the companion of Esteban Puig, the Catalan liberal, legally assassinated last spring in Barcelona by the reactionaries—police, military and clerical."

I had at the time, like everyone else, devoted one day's attention to this matter, which some considered a just punishment, others a martyrdom, and all equally consigned to oblivion shortly after. I was therefore surprised at her description of the meeting in Lausanne, from which she—striking her chest—said she still vibrated.

In order that there should be no prescription and to bring pressure upon the Spanish government, the International Socialist Committee had just organized a monster demonstration.

The assembly, she explained to me, had gathered, orderly, compact, in the rain at the lake's edge. The human tide had risen to the balconies of the villas, to the terraces of the hotels; the curious hung from the roofs. They sold postcards in sets. The subscription lists were covered with signatures. Preceded by their silk emblems, the delegations advanced: the Zurich and Lugano anarchist groups with black banners; the Russian socialist-revolutionaries; the Hindu nationalists, the American Zionists, the General Confederation of Labor, French and Belgian; the employees of the Independent Labor Party and of the Second International sang hymns. The comrades were all there: Rosario, Rakovsky, Vandervelde, Luxemburg, Jaurès, Burns, Thomas, Lippovici. An unforgettable moment! What did it matter to be without a country when she had been received, as she had just been, upon the hearthstone of humanity? Comforted, she would now follow the star of her duty through the most difficult paths, anxious to free herself of that inertia which comes upon one after great sorrows and during which nature regathers her energies. She wished to stay tortured, in her opinions, in her heart, to know no rest, in order that the work to which Puig had given his life should continue and that the Cause should be served. He had left her provided for. She was petite-bourgeoise and naturally too much inclined to a life of ease and comfort, under the soft Southern sky. She was not going to be an amiable widow, devoted to her vines and white rabbits, taking the evening air in a carriage with a lace shawl over her head. She must have the great international combat, the European situation, harsh climates, propaganda campaigns, lectures, to coerce popular attention, to serve the dead man's memory, and to obtain a revision of the infamous sentence.

Enthusiasm leapt from her eyes, from her lips, from the palms of her hands, with some playful, boyish quality that made it extremely attractive. At times she translated her thought solemnly, informing a rotted world of its decadence, "throwing its crimes in its teeth," as she said; at others, carried away by her momentum, she orated full gallop in a headlong and headless ferment of clichés, which didn't however ruin her charm.

The idea of a new society exalted her, fairly making her sweat. The burning Spanish charity was changed into a despotic fervor which only eloquence could draw off. The basis remained a dry, exacting religion, the form as near prayer as possible. Her marvelous credulity served her, encouraged her to romantic sacrilege, and in particular gave her a power of demanding, such as is normally absent in Latin revolutionaries, content usually with so little.

"Man, my life is all in four verbs: serve, know, believe, love."

She carried her thought still further, but before explaining it, she felt constrained to explain her position with regard to the different Spanish political parties. I put so much energy into listening that a slumber engulfed me.

*
* *

We arrived at the frontier.

The lightning accompanied us, annotated by discursive thunder, an unending conversation between peaks. Doña Remedios still clasped her dog which lay with its ears on its mistress' knees and cast a melancholy eye on the small feet adorned with tastefully chiseled buckles and curving like low Empire jewelry.

The day waned, an empty lamp smoking toward the horizon, eau de Cologne monotonously glucked in the hidden fountains of a suitcase; in this rolling domicile of a night, obscured with smoke and smelling of warm leather, my companion read *Chiffonnette's Week Ends*.

Iron-nailed boots on the foot warmers warned us of the approach of the customs officials. Doña Remedios raised her eyes.

"Nothing," she said.

A Southern exciseman attended by a Swiss soldier, his kepi surprisingly bare of "Lift" or some such designation, pointed to a heavy packet still on the rack.

"What's in that game basket?" he queried.

With a gesture, half weariness, half annoyance, she rose, embraced a bouquet of palm leaves tied with a ribbon of scarlet satin. She undid the fastening and in the midst of this foliage disclosed the pale plaster head of a gentleman with empty eyes, not unlike President Carnot.

"There!" she said proudly, "that is the estatue of Esteban Puig, presented to me this afternoon by the B.I.L. (Bureau International de Lausanne). Do we have to pay duty on memories of the dead in order to cross the French frontier?"

She dried a tear on a lace handkerchief the size of a postage stamp.

*

* *

Samuel Pacifico, professor of history in the Lycée Louis-le-Grand, received every Sunday in his lookout, sixth floor, rue Saint-Jacques. We had continued, even after graduation, to visit our former teacher. The author of the *History of the Working Class* was a bashful dwarf, hairy, lined with green veins, with a flavor of the Quartier Saint-Paul; he made his own boots and cut his hair with a machine he himself had invented. He used to drift down the Boul' Mich' grazing the walls, talking to himself, gazing out at the world from a pair of black and gray eyes like photographic plates bathing in yellow developer.

He bore us an affection which had, in the beginning, spared us the tedium of the classroom and which we later preserved and returned to him, never in any ulterior experience having found, as in this chance of childhood, a man willing to corrupt a younger generation no longer worth it. His intelligence, capable of upsetting a state, was at the service of science only. He subjected himself to austere habits and a discipline which he did not wish us to share, holding himself responsible for our happiness. The Jesuits reluctantly sent their pupils to Pacifico's courses. Later, in the École des Sciences Politiques, M. Laguillère-Desveaux interrupted his elegant, colorless lectures to warn us against "the anti-liberal spirit of libertinage in which people in our day undertake the study of sociology."

Pacifico was not present at banquets, never entered a salon, crossed the Seine only to buy rings in the rue de la Paix. He had a collection of these which was disturbing to the ladies. This passion was his only Oriental characteristic. People were afraid of him because he had played in the annals (and also in the darker adventures) of the Third Republic a part which will remain unknown to history, working for his friends and avenging them, pulling, when necessary, mysterious levers which cabinet ministers seldom resisted for more than half a day; never asking anything for himself and having no amusement, save these his weekly receptions.

You could not have opened the folios of Bayle's *Dictionnaire* in the salon of the rue Saint-Jacques at 6 o'clock of a Sunday, space lacking. In this air freighted with tobacco and sealing wax, one found professors in black frock coats, with ready-made ties; coaches, their fingernails stained with acid, a renegade priest, cosmetic'd she-lawyers, a few members of the Draveil communistic colony who carried off coffee spoons, an actress from the Comédie Française, converted to modern art—she had refused the Légion d'Honneur and talked of *going over to the people*.

I was considerably surprised when my train companion entered the circular hall a week later and piloted herself between stacked books and written accumulations. How had I managed not to think sooner that she would appear in this sanctum, this room, modest as the turntable on some line of local interest, although savant and retired and unknown to Paris, like everything that is famous everywhere else. People cross the border and make first for a hotel and this address. Wells, Unamuno, Gorki, Wedekind have signed the Master's album (Shaw wrote simply: G.B.S. Irishman). The big men of Europe had come there to pick up the rudiments of government. It was fitting that in her turn Doña Remedios should continue her work near him whose audacious thought has drowned itself in the deep of wisdom as lieutenant-governors drown powder in sea deeps. Draped in a bachelor's cape lined with white satin, she revolved her large eyes, backed up her answers with a faint pout, mechanically fingering Jaurès' *Socialist History of the French Revolution* as if it were a bargain-sale remnant of dress goods.

"Oh yes, we have met before," she said when Pacifico introduced us. "A storm brought us together."

She recalled the station, the thunder, the dog Trick and its yelping.

"The voyage now appears to me clothed in myth," I said.

"Switzerland has derived from it a splendor which has been denied to it for the past century. The loyalty of the air, the eloquence of the mountain streams, the red elegy of your widowhood, and our dear train with two locomotives bearing us through forests of symbolical pine trees" (Remedios never batted an eyelash) "all these are images with me forever."

She was very satisfactory thus hazarding in Paris the ideas of a swell dressmaker from the Parallelo, all in black, with a hat full of proud feathers, a silver fox fur, a touch of blood in her cheeks, a touch of blood on her hands, living the dream of vengeance while the autumn day faded gently into winter with the chrysanthemums.

Pacifico asked for her autograph.

"A quotation will do?"

When she had put on her spectacles and taken the pen:

"Or a thought, perhaps?" I suggested.

She smiled and held out the book.—"A quotation from our Moratin." And we read:

> *An agreeable woman, she was young and she never thought.*
> *Remedios.*

My embarrassment amused her considerably, and she said it would teach me to make fun of her.

"In the first place, I met you in Helvetia where thought is permissible; now, I assure you, in Paris there is no way of using general ideas; everything is used up in anecdotes."

The Master took Remedios' part and denounced my literary turn of mind. These frivolities took us to dinnertime; we were asked to stay, for these parties had the advantage of not being hostile to laughter, especially after the Collège de France had left the floor free for the younger habitués whom Pacifico called his "prolongation of life." The cooking was good, the wine carefully chosen, our host having entrusted the menage to a housekeeper who had once made the episcopal palace of Toulouse the best inn in the South West.

So a few of us stayed in the vanilla light of the hanging bronze Gothic lamp, surrounded by the deceptive herbage of tapestry on which the portraits of Renan and Berthelot hung facing each other and whose conversation continued above the smoke of turkey and cabbage. Remedios from the top of her too long bust presided over this familial meal.

Pacifico held a glass of sherry toward the gas flame and presented it to Remedios:

"To your health and Puig's glory," he said.

"I thank you and believe you 'on your word.' In rushing to his death, Esteban has only answered the call of the oppressed with heroic heart."

"And now night is again spread over Spain," continued Pacifico.

"It will be that way, hombre, every time someone tries to waken the conscience of a pleb wallowing for centuries" (Remedios pronounced the *b v,* and lisped over the thenturies) "in monarchal ignorance and in *barbarism.* Esteban knew that violence was no use, after the outrages of 1905, and he explained to me that one must work for further ahead. 'We work for results in thirty years, or in fifty years,' he used to say. But as soon as he published his plans, they suppressed him."

A professor of semantics asked for an explanation.

Full of her subject, Remedios looked at us with the defiance of a great pianiste about to attack the "Variations symphoniques." But, doubtless catching my glance, from which all interest and all benevolence were excluded, she avoided the narrative and in a hurried voice set down her conclusions:

"There is nothing but what you know. For travelers, Spain is a country like any other, with lottery tickets, purgative waters, life insurance, members of parliament who kiss each other on the mouth after their speeches, lifts whose floors light up when you step on them. A lovely cloaca. Barcelona is a South American cliché, and at the end of their stems the sleeping cars blossom into hotels that are flowers of mahogany and dark blue velvet. One goes through the streets on metal tracks; they paint as in Schwabing; they only applaud the bullfighters when they've been to Buenos Aires, and they build houses of glass bricks where the autos can go up to the fifth floor.

"Then you turn a corner: the Holy Sacrament—that old coin is still current among us—goes by, everyone kneels (you're fined if you don't kneel), one sees officials with blue silk shoulder belts holding altar candles, followed by officers in soutane and riding boots. The crowded tramcars stop, surrounded by oxcarts and Hispano-Suizas, in order to let these Inquisitors pass, faces of mitred vultures, these sordid old peasant faces projecting from priceless lace, flunkies of a God who has abandoned the humble in order to serve the rich.

"Or else, if a tourist doesn't read the papers and doesn't know there's a strike coming, he is surprised to look out of his hotel windows one morning and see the Guardia Civil in yellow shoulder belts in ambuscade at the street corners waiting for a syndicalist workman to appear. The electric diademed city that had been giving alms to the rest of Spain is now empty as the Sepulcher on Easter morning. The civil population goes to work dandled by hireling rifles. The constitutional guarantees are suspended, and a police of assassins make inquiries in the suburbs that smell of burnt bones, ditch essence, and gum-lac. All this develops in accordance with a detestable ritual. The civil authorities are turned out, a state of siege is proclaimed, in accordance with a telegram said to come from Madrid and which the governor has had in his safe all the time. The power is placed in the hands of the most backward animals on earth—save perhaps for a few Russian governors in the Caucasus. Artillery is posted in the squares, machine guns on the monuments, the troops fire without calling on the mob to disperse. They arrest men in their own houses, they make the searches even at night, they judge them without defending lawyers or witnesses, the read depositions are sheer parody.

"Then in the morning, at dawn, they assassinate in the moats of the citadel. It's over and Truth's veiled for half a century."

She took a cigar, lit it, blew out a long jet of smoke, blue under the hanging lamp, and hummed a tune for the bull's entrance.

"Don't be worried by my excitability. These memories are rather a comfort. People work in Paris but they forget things too soon. One never has time to think about death, that's a Spanish amusement. It's worth thinking of, it helps one to get one's bearings.

"Society has got to break up, or I leave my bones on the ash heap. I don't want to die before I see the great fictions emptied of their hollowness, religion, authority, and the family; with us, more than anywhere else they estill retain their infernal power;

I don't want to die before helping my fellows get free of the 'pobrecity,' of the capitalist and 'padronal' yoke; of all exploiters the Catalans are the harshest, the hardest and most unjust. Oh! the pleasure of an extermination!"

And she hit the table with her fist, not with the thumb inside like a woman, but held properly, like a lock over the fingers. Her bosom shook, as did also the glasses. She was seized with a fit of gaiety and pushing the chair back from the table addressed Pacifico:

"Nourishing father, I thank you for this dinner."

"My red child," he replied, "the place is yours, you are as they say in your country, en casa de Usted."

"For a moment, one interrupts one's plan, fails in one's duty. That is the art, the lure of Paris. But tomorrow we will take up our work, until the prison bars give way, until the glittering and prolific edifice of Espain crumbles."

She was exquisite thus, ardent, strong; at rest she seemed disunited, precious, inept, almost ridiculous. To think in Capital Letters, to be carried to extremes became her, even though, after having sentimentalized, one was amiably ready to punish oneself by regarding her as a role from some Spanish tragicomedy. Watching her under the hanging lamp, consuming herself in extremist speeches, settled in on her calm avoirdupois, on her weighty body with its heavy binding muscles like those of a well-fed female cashier, one hesitated, or one refused, to share her enthusiasm. But she seemed still less alluring when she subsided into a simple young woman, agreeable and of a permanent freshness. One thought by turns that she was an eagless or a milk-fed hen; in either case, a pleasant effigy, without any prodigious talent, with no mark of destiny on her. Unhappiness had traced no bitterness on her puffy infantile nose, on her ample lips, no groove on her low forehead, beneath which the pupils were stretched over round eyes, filled with a glow both permanent and inoffensive.

I continued to study her. She was freed from all belief, liberated from human burdens and celestial hypotheses; one didn't expect less of her. But what one liked at the end of it all in this rebel was the decorum, the honesty of the sentiments, a Catholic heredity mixed with the Spanish bourgeoise's respectful acknowledgment of the male—which comes down, perhaps, from the

75

Moors. We all of us felt it there, sitting about her; but we all, as it were, wanted to put her faith to the test, were on the lookout for her giving way, believing in a sentimental anarchic escapade much more than in a vocation.

"Remedios," said one guest in rising, "is a purely domestic eclogue. A siren in the waters of Marxism."

"It would be interesting to look into her future," admonished Pacifico, who was not inoculated against occultism.

Each one summarized:

"I think she will end in the violence of a period bloody in spite of her."

"She will marry a retired toreador for his figure and keep a hotel in Algeciras."

"She will go on a lecture tour in the Argentine, if she doesn't end in the cinema."

"Femme de lettres?"

"No. I believe she is chaste."

The evening was no longer serious. A friend of Pacifico's childhood, an aged gentleman with painted cheeks who played chess and mended old lace, offered to tell the cards. But we preferred the game of putting down a list of qualities and defects, each for himself, counting from 0 to 20, and were now scribbling on our knees. The old gentleman having gone to the piano where he rendered the overture for the *Galant Indies*. The October wind scattered white wood ash over the carpet.

Remedios moistened her pencil in perplexity, wanted to know the difference between sensuality and temperament, vowed there was one word in Spanish, and that she at any rate couldn't for herself see any difference between them. Pacifico, out for precision, managed to get the absolute of "goodness" changed into kindliness. Someone protested shrilly against the omission of "snobisme." Some cheated, others, overcome with remorse, erased their notes, or after an examination of conscience, allowed themselves a more complimentary mark. Remedios proceeded with hesitation, rubber in hand, struggling with concentrated sincerity. I asked could one give oneself more than 20.

There was no sound but that of the housekeeper clearing the table, the creaking of furniture, and the even movement of a pendulum. When the slips were full, Pacifico read over the list again and each one with courage or shame avouched the grade he had given himself.

"Do we know ourselves?" said Pacifico. "One does, remarkably, just that. Even the youngest are, I should note, still subject to errors, but among the elders, no more illusions."

We then proceeded to the second part of the game, taking someone else's sheet and correcting it according to our own estimate.

"But you know nothing about me!" said Remedios as I laid hold of her moral inventory.

I replied that I would endeavor to guess and that I had, moreover, drunk out of her glass in the dining car without her having noticed it.

A lot of time has gone by since that happy Sunday. I have kept Remedios' table, with my corrections. I offer the precious document which now, despite the dryness of statistics, appears to me full of confessions:

REMEDIOS.

Quality or defect.	Her estimate.	My rectification.
Beauty	18	14
Charm	9	17
Elegance	20	8
Intelligence	2	7
Genius	3	?
Sensibility	8	19
Business sense	1	18
Sensuality	0	19
Temperament	2	15
Modesty	20	10
Political acumen	19	3
Judgment	8	4
Wit	10	10
Religious sense	0	20
Snobisme	7	17
Luck	0	19
Good luck	1	18
Will power	16	5
Egoism	19	4
Love of food	18	18

"If you like, Remedios, we might dine some evening, without dressing, then go to the cinema."

"With pleasure. I don't like being alone. There is a mysterious rapping on my shutter every evening, and a nun appears in my wardrobe whenever I open it to take out a shirtwaist."

"And: *'I am afraid to die when I sleep alone.'* "

"Whose is it?"

"Verlaine's, but it ought to be Baudelaire's."

"Come for me Tuesday at 7:30. Hotel du Mexique, rue Servandoni."

I had to wait for Remedios in a hall full of palms, on a blue cane armchair until the cuckoo clock marked a quarter to nine. The linoleum-covered table d'hôte had been cleared for two hours. The ecclesiastical boarders had played with the cat, read the notices in *La Croix,* the piquet had subsided. They were going to bed. Remedios at last descended, clicking with jewelry, in a cloak of black Liberty silk, half open like a doorway leading to an intimate and well-padded room; a grand décolleté, she was holding her key and her candlestick. A comb of carved tortoise shell surmounted her, a foot high; it poked into the roof of the carriage. This vision impelled me to give up all idea of a cabaret. In my thought I ransacked the Grand Boulevards to find a restaurant which one could, so adorned, enter.

Despite my precautions, we did not wholly escape attention.

"What do you say to my having only water and vegetables?"

"Remedios, woman of the Great Evening, and of great evening parties, do be serious. Will you have it natural or sweet?"

Between the salt and pepper she deposited a pair of twisted white gloves, a velvet handbag on which was embroidered in brilliants

REMEDIOS
SIN DIOS

and a fan of green ostrich plumes.

"I will take oysters," she said in a resigned tone, "and you can put one in a bag—for my Japanese goldfish. And I will take a slice of mutton for Trick. You dine with a woman who was rich this morning and who is now penniless. I told you, I think, in the train—that spontaneous need to talk about oneself that we call sympathy—that Esteban Puig had left me provided for. He left me a little house property in Biarritz. The fact is, I am supposed to have come in for a good deal more. I was worried about it. This morning I bought *El Debate*, a Jesuit paper, in the Boul' Mich' and saw what the enemy could make out of it. I have seen my lawyer and had him draw up a formal act of renunciation which will appear tomorrow in *L'Humanité*. All of Puig's money will go straight to his Socialist Institute. Now you know why I'm a pauper."

She smiled, stirring her wine with a fork.

"No, this renunciation is not meritorious. To have taken it at all was wrong. I shall always keep Puig's real gifts. He found me, chose me, raised me to his own level when I was only a pupil-teacher in a suburban school. He made me read, made me think, to the eve of his death he was anxious to create a companion worthy of him. He was twenty years older than I was, tall, with a head like a rock, the eyes of a basilisk, but the lower part of his face, and his hands, were quiet and full of wisdom. So he appeared to me when he came one day to ask me to take an evening class for workingmen's children. His voice trembled and seemed to come out of hiding. He said that he needed me. His face was white as an altar cloth. And I followed him."

She was in that solid décolleté, her high breast spilling a little over the corsage, as from a cup overfull.

"Where's your dress from?"

"Worth. *Orient Evening.* So much the worse . . . From now on I'll copy my dresses from the pictures in the *Vanguardia* supplement."

She continued:

"Imagine. The Socialist Institute, Puig was the soul of it. He created it in 19— on an entirely new pedagogic basis—at least for Espain—you can see what a revolution it was—coeducation not only of sexes, but of all social classes together. Moreover, with moral and material hygiene, truth taught without reward or punishment, science without religion, a proper proportion of manual and mental work. In short the admirable educational edicts of your Convention; Lavoisier's ideas, Puig said, put into practice, as they never have been in France. Reclus, Kropotkin helped him. I have their splendid letters in a hatbox. But to create this meant loosing the combat of light against darkness, and one can't do that without being punished. Puig was beaten. In our country you can't take the children away from the Church people who want to turn every man into a saint."

She stopped, fascinated by her pocket mirror.

"How black I am! Why?"

"A woman's conscience is her complexion."

"Rage gone to my liver. Excuse me; but one has to get these things out. Even though the headwaiter is listening in terror, do you know the end of Portet's oration for Puig?" Then declaiming: " 'The supposed son of one of those numerous gods whom men have created is condemned for having wished to proclaim himself king. He is about to die. Born, like all gods, out of ignorance, out of fear, he falters in the presence of death, he loses confidence, trembles and cries out "Father, why hast thou forsaken me?" On the other hand, behold Esteban Puig, son of free thought, of ethics without sanction, he too is condemned to death. Will he falter? Will he lose his free vision? No. He stiffens and he falls, crying *"L'Internationale!"* ' "

Remedios' eyes are black, or gray, or blue. How can one know? All eyes are all colors. My pleasure suddenly sinks. I reach out my hands like splints and seize her hand fractured at the wrist by a bracelet of square-set sapphires. I want to go further, but everything seems to take root. It is a dream. Nothing is lacking, not even the feeling of teeth going into one's heart.

"Remedios?"

"Please?"

"Please let me love you."

I had not chosen my moment, but I had made up my mind, the night before, to deliver this confession. She pleased me immeasurably and, each day, more.

"You should be quite wrong," she said shrugging her chubby shoulders jerkily, and thus annihilating her already short neck.

"I am telling you principally in order that I shouldn't be."

Speaking of love had brought back flavor to the coffee and restored that equilibrium which brings us the sympathy of the purveyors and the friendship of destiny.

"It's because, when I am not violent, and weak and submissive to the dominations of tendencies, my unpleasantness has, Remedios, no limit."

"So I had noticed," she said. "And to be equally frank, I tell you that I will never love again. My life, in that respect, is finished. Physical love is merely a sublime debauch, which time may, if necessary, replace. But the deep attachment of two hearts once broken?"

Upon which she cited some fatly sentimental Andalusian proverb that took the charm from her face.

After a silence:

"I shall make my living teaching Spanish."

"Will you take me for one of your pupils?"

"The first and dearest."

The restaurant door turned its paddle wheel of pink silk in the pool of the curved glass panes. Tables were emptying. Women came down the stairs in their bright-lined evening cloaks, like statues in colored niches. Men found effusively a friend or hat.

In the warm room Remedios gave off an aroma like mulled wine. The last diners, also, distilled a gentle contentment. The wine waiter was immortal. A lady drank with uplifted finger, concluding:

"It is good, it leaves a faint flavor."

The radiators cooled with their joints creaking and thumping.

Remedios pushed back her plate, her glass, took up her rougestick and wrote a jota on the tablecloth.

"Preliminary notations. The alphabet is A, B, C, D, E, F, G, H, I, J . . . that is the jota. No, it isn't a dance, it's the first difficulty that waits you south of the Pyrenees."

I tried for a full minute.

"I'm surprised at your progress," said Remedios, flatteringly. "Now let us choose a phrase where the *r* and the *j* are well differentiated:

"EL PAJARITO DE LA CAJA ROJA."

"Yes, Remedios, and what does that purring all mean?"

"It means the little bird in the red cage."

"That's you, Remedios."

It is late. We rise. The restaurant is empty. I love her for life. While she goes to the cloakroom, I return to our table and lick her spoon surreptitiously.

*

* *

I had patiently trained my tongue to roll the *r*'s on my teeth, whence I plucked it back sharply against the glottis, for an undamaged pronunciation of the jota. All the way to the rue Servandoni I forced myself through the phrase which Remedios had taught me the night before last.

I found a note for me at her hotel. She had left France the previous evening by the Barcelona express. The red cage was empty. There remained the detestable hall decorated with lizard skins, with tinted glasses, and a cat which ate some sort of cerebral pulp from a dish of false Rouen ware. The autumn day was finishing itself without agitation, under the dais of an orange-hued storm, enlarged with cloud layers, such as those wherewith the lyric painters load our façades. I remained in the Luxembourg like a monolith, crushed by a two days' habit, stuck fast in a new fidelity. I had prepared myself to find Remedios again, to besiege her with puerile emotions as if one were curing the hiccoughs, to ask one thousand grammatical questions, to create for her fantastic fantasies without revealing my plan, which was to rivet her attention upon me, to persuade her that all the finesse of Paris, the breath of the Seine, the genius of the Saint-Michel fountain when the water overflows as in a bathtub if one goes to sleep, the avowal of theater ushers behind the program, "It costs me one franc," the readymade pleasures in a private room in a restaurant, the liberal existence of department stores, when the samples are unfurled in small waves from central hall newel posts amid a splendor of orchids, that all these were but the varied form of one love. A love to which the cafés also lent their assistance and 7:45 p.m. (hour of Western Europe) its ineffable relaxation.

By this uncomplicated leave-taking I saw her, on the contrary, acquitted; in most peaceful possession of herself; and, forever, distant. Before night had fallen, while the only stars were as yet those on the tram wires, it was evident to me that my subjugation was assured, that a confiscation of my happiness had been suddenly affected, even after the legal hour of sunset. Why this sudden intestate departure? Was not Spain forbidden her? Had she not perhaps hidden the truth from me, embarked for the headlong pleasures of Italy; or gone, for exhibitionism or humility, to America?

It had been Spain, quite certainly, as a post card came next day from the frontier. One observed thereon the quays of Port-Vendres, with a row of huge wine casks, a view of the Mairie, dominated by a fort. The back of the card bore: "Command of destiny," though the proud brevity of this already Spanish inscription was somewhat corrected by a handwriting like a servant girl's and the farewell: "Un bonjour de Port-Vendres." I hoped that Remedios would not be permitted to cross the frontier, but a few days later Pacifico said she had reached Barcelona.

Paris was inundated by the rains of a slackened November. The asphalt reflected the house fronts up to the roofs. The splashes of mist about the street lights diluted a sort of rose-colored dust . . . Along submerged sidewalks the deformed trees gave themselves up to the wind. By the sewer mouths, at night, one heard rumbles of the torrents under the streets. My regret for Remedios declined to diminish.

Our first meetings seemed like fate's admonition that our lives should not pass in mutual ignorance. I reconstructed my series of symptoms. I had first loved her voice, broken by public meetings, her short hands, made still shorter by mittens, her assassin's thumb, her blend of adventures and lethargies, her anarchic enterprise; then her abbreviated stock of ideas, the repertoire of her sufferings, her kindness and the continual diversion afforded by her taste for pleasure, her natural dispositions to duty and the insurrections which threw her out of her destiny. I saw her again, irresponsible, romantic, and smiling. Our meeting would be one of those events which Remedios judged on evidence, designed to trouble her peace of mind, but inevitable? Omens had their share in this process, the shapes in clouds and in coffee grounds became threatening. The solitude of the evenings or even of mornings when there was too much sun for me to accept the situation and live prudently encouraged me to pack up. The papers announced grave reactionary measures in Catalonia. I could not bear the thought that far from me Remedios was dashing toward some catastrophe, and I took the evening express in my turn.

*

* *

Now take a sanded arena, an even strand where the forces of shadow and light contend equally. A circus of azure where the impetuous sun advances, without meeting the spread capa of storm cloud. A crowd separates the two empty arenas. Like a frame of somber wood it encloses these two mirrors which throw back the glare at each other. The warm air distributes a million pale flakes of light on the juxtaposed faces, makes scattered sounds vibrate, and gathers them into harmony. Is one of these spots, is one of these sounds Remedios? Has she like myself followed this long-trailing crowd?

It is a press gala, and eight Sottomayor bulls are promised by the turbulent posters. In an hour the whole city has poured itself into this Moorish basin. Carefully, I sift the benches like corn. I depopulate the stands of everything that is not a brilliant and fluent mouth, a well-designed body in a foulard gown, eyes readable as a notice board. Are you there, Remedios, precious commodity, useful substance? Perhaps, but unrecognizable, being no longer the unreasonable, emotive image, the flame which one could have instantly isolated in the gray Paris crowd; from henceforth but one gleam amid these thousand flexible others, one of these bodies satiated by siestas, swollen with sugar, excited by vows and omens; a Spanish woman.

Here the booted Guardia Civil. Here the military band in espadillas. The president verbalizes from his box. Bonbonlike ladies give him attention. He hurls his gestures at the crowd, like handfuls of pennies. Strident whistles ring out and subside. The president rises. He shakes his handkerchief so violently that it uncorks a brass clarion at the other end of the arena. The clarion opens the bull door, showing a dusky passageway terminating in a square patch of blue.

The bull has plunged into the light. Stops timidly at the edge of the shadow. His coat is dirty, flanks mottled. His horns are white with wallplaster. He is alone, the solitary target upon which the two hemicycles of seats converge. A mare kicking the palisade attracts him. He moves toward her. She is a pumice-colored wreck, her belly sewn up like a poor woman's petticoats, her legs waver under the weight of the upholstered picador shaking his lance. The bull pauses an instant, and bellows. Caught by the fat glitter of the menacing steel, he advances, his nose grazing the ground. The picador's calves stiffen. The lance goes into the bull's shoulder. The horns sink into the mare's belly with a squish. She seems to jump, and stays there suspended, while the bull blind with the warm blood rummages about in her belly. Then she comes down, like an old wall dragging the rider with her, stuffed in his armor of mattresses. The picador's head emerges from the harness and tripes, the tasseled hat has fallen off it, and one sees his fat scared face, a Capuchin's, shining. The mare staggers up and distributes her entrails round the bullring. Other animals lie along by the palisade, unsaddled, their bones sticking out still further, and their yellow teeth showing.

Remedios? None of these fans pushes the air against that dear throat that used, in Paris, to be so deeply grooved by her veil. No eyebrow is as pitch-black as the ones she used to smooth with a little brush—the sort they use to dress pastry. No one near me speaks her hoarse heart-capturing speech. Remedios hasn't come. Remedios doesn't like bloodshed.

The bull is now baited by silver-clothed men set out like chess pawns. One by one they open their wings, fly, come to rest in front of his sanguine horns. One hangs a cloak over the bull's rump, and his socks stick out, stupid pink, under this petticoat. Another holds up a flag, very high, with blood dried onto it in somber splotches. He drags the capa on the ground like a fishnet, or opens it out into a curtain. He pulls the curtain aside, and bang! a man has cut through the sunlight, leaving the bull four tin-foiled banderillas, a silver flower along which the blood oozes, already black.

The bull grows logy. He now belongs to the gold-covered man. A compact mass of mutterings rises by degrees from the crowd, breaks into a thousand sounds at the first clever move. The killer is small. His hair and slippers are varnished. The bull tears his cloth rag and the silk of his sleeves. Grows tired. His head droops lower and lower, marking the ground with his slobber. The man takes three steps backward, wipes the sweat from his blue and yellow face, throws off his hat with a theatrical gesture; he is bald. He rises on his toes, like a tenor. There is an "ajh!" quickly stifled, a leap backward; he waits, hands on his hips, a smile crinkling his thin cheeks. He makes a sign to the crowd to postpone its pleasure for a moment. The bull retreats sideways, its nostrils in the sand, its legs bending, it falls on its knees, the feet stiffen, the head jerks backward.

The president grants the bull's ears to the matador.

There is nothing left in the arena but trodden space, a mingling of footmarks and hoofmarks round a stain.

Am I sick from this anise-perfumed afternoon, or from a sentimental strike, or from this hideous butchery?

*
*　*

My search lasted two days. Finally I got her phone number from the Instituto Socialista. Her voice. She gave me a rendezvous for next morning, 7 a.m., in the suburbs.

I tried, vainly, to sleep. My windows opened on a flat boulevard bordered with palm trees. Children played there until two in the morning, shoveling electric sand under the arc lights, squabbling in the middle of a night of which other European offspring know only the margins. The electric ads glared. The celebration of soap covered one house front with a blood-flux. The house disappeared in shadow, to reappear in blue, in green, like a favorite dancer replying to succeeding encores in a succession of different-hued shawls. Above this domestic effusion shaved four times a minute by the lighthouse the citadel of Montjuich continued its rocky, sinister vigil.

The square emptied at three. The trente et quarante rooms still kindled the first floors. One saw chandeliers, floorboards; players came out and rested their elbows on the plush-bordered balcony rail while the cards were being reshuffled. The coachmen below played in their cabs. With the first efforts of dawn over the ocean the barbers stopped trepanning their clients with hair oil, hid their hot-water pans under towels, and the town entered a brief repose.

A little later a taxi came to take me to Vich Park, where Remedios had given me rendezvous. In Plaza Colon the brotherhood of beggars slept stretched over two iron chairs each. There were a hundred of them, with black faces, their feet wrapped in last evening's newspapers, under pachydermatous palms, catching lice in their sleep. Among them a gentleman, in evening clothes, a flower in his buttonhole, having renounced his domicile, snored with his mouth open. The taxi proceeded through the suburb of Arguelles, the quarter of cotton-exchange profiteers. I wondered whether I was yet awake, there were nothing but villas, twisted like marshmallows, receiving their light through mailed windows, protected by metallic seafoliage, by zinc bindweed painted trail pink and green. Rubber houses sank beneath warped armor-plating, the street ran through their yawning portals and mounted with gentle slope to the roofs. Porter's lodges hung on their flanks like goiters, the chimneys bulgy with varicose veins sprouted from wall tops where the chimera struggled amid the clumps of wrought-iron iris. When the architects had exhausted themselves, the avenues were indicated only by sign posts, astray in the vacant lots. Here and there between kitchen gardens a private house still reared its finicky birthday-cake silhouette, grated with almond-shaped bits of glass, bristling with boulders and ill-assorted burnt almonds. Finally the cab stopped before a ceramic terrace, adorned with candied fruit and held up by twelve inebriate monoliths. This plate was evidently intended to serve also as a roof, for varnished tiles perforated with saltcellar holes emerged arbiform from it. I entered a path which writhed like a cut worm, and followed its spirals to a checker-board pavillion, where, smiling amid the aloes, Remedios waited. She was nearly naked under her dustcoat (lilac colored, bought at Valentine's, the rubber king's). Her oiled hair reflected the heaven. She rolled her aquarium eyes toward me, compressed her lips into that pointless kiss, a pout.

"Sympathetic, are you satisfied?"

"I am in a dream. I adore you."

She patted me on the shoulder, then on the back, thus manifesting her Spanish pleasure at seeing me once again, and by one of these caresses which one still sees at the Théâtre Français in classic comedy.

"How can I explain the sacrifices I have made in renouncing my resistance," she said. "You come at a terrible moment, when I ought to see no one, but heaven . . . This is the Vich Park, presented to the city by a Catalan who made his fortune in Chile. Bagatelle and Luna Park thrown together. Confess that it is idyllic; these eslopes, these aloes, these designs in blown glass, and the e-steam orchestra in the grotto every evening. I am happy, as in the popular tango:

> I wish I were a bee,
> I'd die among the flowers.

"Instead of that one must estruggle always. Oh, I can perfectly well tell you now that it isn't what I was made for. I'm party secretary of a liberal league, honorary president, along with Anatole France, traveling delegate, lecturer, propagandist as well. But what I really like is breakfast in my dressing gown, and to have a little ladies' maid, and birds, and to have the coiffeur come in to do my hair, and to go to esleep in estrong arms, and to have my chocolate in bed, go to the cinema, at the heure de l'apéritif, the función-vermouth as they call it here, and to have dinner with my sisters, among my nephews and nieces, and to find roses near my bed when I come home. Let this confession go down, between us, to the grave. Now go. I am not sure I have not been followed, even though I have come straight from bed at this hour. Take the evening train back to France."

"I came all the way here to see you."

She was insistent:

"There will be, perhaps, a general estrike in Barcelona tomorrow. All foreigners will be suspect: they will shoot savagely. I can't say anything more."

"My love for you, Remedios, is my sole preoccupation, and the wish to seduce you my only error. If I am thrown into danger with you it will not be from imprudence or from gallantry, nor for a joke, but because the need of seeing you keeps me here."

Having spoken, I drew her to me. She deposited rice powder and dried milk of pearls on my clothing, became tender, put on her spectacles.

From the height of our Calvary, surrounded by maniac hummocks on which the heliotrope reproduced insignia of the order of Alfonso XII, between crenelations bolstered with breastplates, the city showed through the tense air, purified, like an architect's design sent in for competition. Only the sea was encumbered with a misty amalgam, sticking it to the sky. The funicular began to move, a dynamo purred.

"That's Barcelona waking up," said Remedios, "luxurious homes, obedient trams, municipal embellishments, a complete industrial eloquence, but you don't know what the hours of blood are: hacked shutters, burst pipes, and a single stain under my windows, estroked by the sunlight; the body of a little girl killed coming out of school, estretched on the ground, her head eaten by flies." (When she spoke rapidly Remedios shot out little particles of silvery saliva that shone in the sun for an instant.)

"Yes, you monkey. It was less than a year ago, it began by a meeting to protest against reservists being sent to Morocco, that cancer that gnaws at Spain's vitals. The Capitanía General was on the watch, before that station there, smoking like soup, to the right; and where they had pulled up the rails to keep out reinforcements from Valencia and Madrid. It was a Wednesday. They tore up the paving stones and cut down the trees. The sack of the convents started at noon. First St. Martin de los Provenzales, if I remember right. Puig had gone out the night before and hadn't come home. At medianoche I risked going out. The crowd was moving toward the center, after sacking the armories. I learned that Puig was on duty at the Casa del Pueblo. The convents of the Marists, of St. Anthony, of St. Paul, and the Congreganist churches were burnt one after another. They burnt off forty-nine of 'em. The mitrailleuses on the top of Columbus' estatue made a clearing. The infantry refused to fire. The Jesuits of Sarria, that barracks there by the gasworks, defended themselves with rifles. The Montjuich forts finally got the range on the revolutionary committee. From my room I heard dull explosions, bursting of reserve bombs, syndicalist or clerical, in their hiding places. Then the reinforcements arrived. General Santiago had terrifying proclamations pasted up. The ringleaders got to the Pyrenees. The detonations became rarer and finally stopped . . . Barcelona was once more what you see there, a city of money, and vice, the town of brothels full of girls underage, of obscene photographs, instruments of orthopedic pleasure, hiding her old inquisitionist soul behind illuminated advertisements, with her convents and her banks fortified, with doors on her apartment buildings such as you'd find on a safe, with her fireproof cellars, her confessionals defended from the poor by the same gilded gratings. During this time Puig had been arrested and locked in, up there.

"They had him. At last they had their hands on this dangerous anarchist. No civil lawyer could get through the door to him. And you remember all outraged Europe, all the justicist eyes turned toward the casemate where the greatest heart awaited without a tremor. Esocrates, Jesus, le Chevalier du Barreau, Bismarck, Ravachol, all the great adventurers of thought have died like this. I never saw him living again. Puig wrote to me every day. I know it, but his letters never came to me. They put me into close confinement in a cabin of the *Pelayo*, that old battleship always handy to serve as a jail, sleeping its crocodile sleep in the harbor here.

"Look, they are running up all the little flags, today they'll put up tin-foiled triumphal arches through all the city; there'll be a candle in every window this evening, because the king is coming tomorrow to review the troops before they go off to Tetuán. It will be the same thing, all over again, till . . ."

The good homely odor of chocolate rose in the morning air.

With fixed gaze, Remedios sucked her pendant. Then she spoke as if in her sleep.

"Puig was put in chapel at six in the evening. He stayed awake all night refusing to kneel, standing up between two Brothers of Charity . . . He died shot in the back. For a whole day after he was on view in his black pine coffin, his head wrapped in bandages, his face bloodless, a wound in the throat plugged with lime."

Suddenly she threw her arms round my neck.

"What a kid I am, amn't I?"

*
* *

I wanted to open the window, but Remedios snatched the curtain and pulled it shut with a swish.

"Because of that chap on patrol?"

I had for some time been noticing a very tall stoop-shouldered man with a pretty porcelain face wrapped in beard, who was watching us.

"Yes, it's José Salt."

"Police?"

"No."

"Jealous?"

"It's too bad. Salt used to be professor of history at the Institute. He helped Puig with intelligence, envy, and vanity. Then I gave a course, as you know, and became Puig's companion. Salt fell in love with me, and lost his balance. He spied on us, followed us, flooded us with anonymous letters, probably denounced us to the police; in short, became so queer that Puig in spite of his gentleness and self-control got into a row with him, after which Salt had to leave. He was in the Argentine when things happened. I found him here on my return, avoiding me, and dedicating me poems. He has restarted his lectures—sermons of an illuminatus, which the students avoid—he passes his nights in churches and takes cocaine. Yesterday he came up to me in the street and asked me to live with him, and, as I tried to get away, he said that tomorrow he would make a bouquet of my favorite flowers, and that he would put a bomb in it and throw it into the king's carriage on his return from the review."

"It's these romantic applications that make anarchy unbearable. It ought to be, to begin with, an exact science. But since they have taken to neglecting theology the Spaniards have lost all method."

"That's true, sympathetic love, you babble like a chaffinch . . ."

I heard my neck break; I found, at the edge of my lips, teeth that were not my own; I was warmer than in full sunshine; it was impossible to breathe; next to my eyes I saw a single eye blazing, it transfixed me, hurt me, and went out.

"Who could change me so?" said Remedios after this caress. "I assure you that it isn't a passade, that's what you call it in Paris, isn't it? No, I assure you, I have no taste for pleasure, but I saw you unhappy, I couldn't help it."

91

"It's before it, I'm the sad animal . . ."

"I felt the same way once before when we dined together in Paris, and you let me ask the Tzigane for the stanzas of Lakmé. I remember:

C'est que Dieu de nous se retire.

At that moment we heard the lobster claws being cracked; it was as if my heart were being crushed. You see, there is something beating beneath it. In France your ex-votos are ballots, palmes académiques, dentist's diplomas. In Espain around the estatues of the Virgin they hang hearts, clusters of hearts . . ."

"And," I added, "sore eyes, fibromas, and, notably, at Toledo a set of wax gonads (male)."

"Besides, why should I appeal to fate, aren't we together again? Such a long time, we have been parted . . ."

"And you've grown thinner," I flatteringly continued.

"That means you'll love me forever?"

"Naturally."

"I wish you were a cat," said Remedios, playing with my watch chain, "and that you would never leave me. I would put you in a little basket during the day time, and take you out in the evening, and then you would resume your human form."

She had on a satin waist with large childish dots on it, a sailor collar and tie of white crepe. I wanted to bite her little feet and to prevent their swinging so in the air. What a heredity of seated ancestry must have been needed for it! We are alone in the creamery, with the flies. The half of a Holland cheese, looking like a severed breast, shares its glass cover with a raw ham, smelling of suet and already turning black.

"When do we restart lessons? The irregular verbs?"

Remedios perused the lines of my eyes. I could see nothing but her round nose all over powder, projecting from her plump skin.

"I thought you were over-sensitive," she explained, "and capable of a great deal of affection. You must know me better. I am, you know, overnervous."

I opened the window all the same, so she could call for help if I murdered her.

"They haven't often accused you of having a withered heart. And yet you aren't very expressive."

Her bust is too long; a single sigh stands perpendicular in it and furnishes the whole creamery.

The sidewalk runs along a deformed quay. Barcelona is a horrible city. Women go by, their eyebrows are too thick, their rumps too large, they are followed by emaciated Jesuits who go along holding each other by their little fingers. Behind and over it all is Montjuich, which one will certainly never escape. The abrupt rock with palm trees stuck into its cracks like body hair, with bouillabaisse restaurants hanging about it like watch fobs. Through the other window the landscape exhibits a vendor of dyed feathers and, further off, a modern cathedral, in the style of Soller, four towers of ferroconcrete set round one barrel organ. Remedios grows smaller. She becomes a normal companion. She has set aside the parade of authority whereby she asserted herself in Switzerland, in France. Her country diminishes her. Is that why she wanted to be without one? She had been Love and Glory. And here she was, become convenient, shimmering, flexible, a household utensil. She submerged me with glances for me alone, glances which said, "After all one must live, and as well as one can." She forgot the dead man, seized the living one, and used the same expression: "her sacrifice." She believed it—not without reason. I disliked myself for not feeling grateful. Perhaps the dotted waist and white crepe tie had something to do with it? How she had pleased me in Paris, in full mourning! There had been that silver veil for interviews. She ascended the rue St. Jacques like a Calvary. And the buzz of the rubbernecks behind her! I believed there, as always, in the exceptional. Today, without hypocrisy toward myself, without irony toward her . . .

"This evening," she said, "we will go up to Tibidabo by the funicular. I will bring Trick. We will dine à la carte. There's a view out to the Palma lighthouse. I will let my head sink eslowly onto your shoulder. We will set sail for the land of conventional, unheroic dreams. I'll bring a nightgown."

Her jet earrings trembled and acquiesced from each ear.

*

* *

93

I had room 217. It was new and smelt of varnish. A cockroach traversed the carpet, without haste. A forgotten ace of clubs lay in one of the drawers. I ordered dinner for two. At that moment there was a distant explosion. The electricity gave out, and I lighted three candles.

I opened the window; a smell of shrimp soup and washing rose from the courtyard. I counted the flowers on the bedspread. I polished my oxydized toilet bottles with the curtains. Then I hid my slippers. At last, mechanically, I put flowers into a waterless vase, as they do in the theater.

Remedios wanted me to be a cat in a little basket. She had promised me a cigarette case with an enameled top representing a nude blonde by the seashore. She had sent the bust of Esteban Puig to my hotel—why?—with its upturned eyeballs, all wrapped in oilcloth. I had had to put it under the bed. What should I do with it? Would I end by resigning myself to . . . ? To live. Then to live alone, or to accept other people as one finds them. Why did the newspapers here use their front page for funeral notices? Sending up this sinister quotidian wail?

I made resolutions. I must have an enthusiasm. I ought to be torn by emotion, I ought to be more emotive. Perhaps a chronic excitement. Remedios is incomparable, a ray of light sprouts from her forehead.

Tired of waiting, I dined. Every twenty minutes the funicular announced its arrival with a thud which caused the mountain to tremble. This was followed by the sound of a waterfall. My anxiety doubled each time. I pricked up my ears. But Remedios was not yet in that car. I daren't explain her lateness or face the fact that she mightn't come, for fear of arousing contrary forces which would prevent her arrival. With my whole heart I desired Remedios, I longed to see her shut in with me between these four smooth sanitarium walls. I forgot that, that morning, I would have given anything to be back in Paris.

Little by little I forced myself to think that Remedios certainly wouldn't come, but that the night would be, nevertheless, bearable, pleasant, stretched out catty-cornered on the bed.

The hotel was eight hundred meters up. The sounds of the countryside didn't yet reach it, the sounds from the city ceased coming. They each in their different way induce sleep, which was denied me. There was nothing for me but waiting.

I lay down with my clothes on. About two o'clock the people in the next room, who had been talking volubly, vigorously, without rest, ordered an entrecôte and manzanilla. Then a child yowled, announcing the dawn. Another infant emitted an answering wail.

I had left the door ajar and trembled at every noise. I fell asleep a hundred times to the minute. The telephone rang in the corridor, and the hall waiter, asleep under his red-shaded lamp, did nothing to stop it. The panels of the imported British furniture split cracklingly in the darkness. At every start I found the pillow next to me swollen and cold and the boundless room lit only by the moon which an obliging mirror reflected into the dusty water of a fire-bucket.

Then all at once I slept.

It wasn't till the morning after that I learned the cause of the explosion and heard of the arrest of Remedios.

Turkish Night

⌇ The Simplon-Orient dragged its triweekly public through the gloom as usual. The usual French dressmakers and, less elderly, milliners were returning to Constantinople with a new lot of models; at Laroche the perfume of Paris began to fade and the tenacious Oriental odors, rose and peppery bergamot, reasserted themselves. Officials' wives flitted in the corridor with six infant children who wouldn't be properly put to bed this side of Bombay. Officers of the État-major, in police caps, strode up the station platforms during the stops, stretching their short, authoritative legs. French hearts are wholly hidden by the multitude of their decorations. The English slept late, whistled in the conveniences, where they stayed in relays until the water and towels ran out. Israelite-Spanish families from Salonika, returning after clarifying their complexions at Vichy, kept to their bunks all day with their clothes on, stretched on the unmade bedding, beneath swaying flasks of Chianti hung from the electric light fixtures. Then after a tedium they and the rest of us slept to the rattle of axles and the steel castanet springs. Snores. We beat on the mahogany panels to drive back the bedbugs. The conductor snoozed at the end of the corridor, on a cushion stuffed with contraband lire, dinars, drachmas, Rumanian leis, and £T, his alpaca tunic stuffed also with little folded papers full of jewels.

The train shook the loose glass of Gothic Swiss railway stations. For twenty-nine minutes the Simplon offered its large iron symphony. Then the banked roads and rice fields of Piedmont. Then a station leading off into nothing, a great cistern of silence and shadows that was Venice. In the morning a zinc-colored north wind overbent the Croatian corn in the plains. Pigs, striped black and white as with racing colors, betrayed the presence of Serbia; they were apparently devouring the corpse, or rather the wheels and an alarm signal, of a car which lay still derailed in a ditch. After rivers came yet other rivers that we crossed on rickety trestles beside the ruined piers of older bridges which had been destroyed in retreats. At Vinkovci we got rid of the velvet Rumanians, velvet eyes, velvet mustaches, daughters in undershirts plaiting their hair in the gelid darkness by the glimmer of half-frozen candles. After Sofia, pimentos hung drying across the house fronts. Oriental sun beat upon the Bulgar plains, ox-ploughs obtruded a symbolic prosperity as depicted upon the Bulgars' postage stamps and their money. At last, after the desert of Thrace, under a sky full of constellations lacking a polestar, with the disfigured Bear no longer recognizable at the low edge of the horizon, the Sea of Marmora stretched before us through a breach in the Byzantine wall.

*

* *

The boat wouldn't go till tomorrow morning. I had the evening before me. The hotel was unbearable: sneaky faces, loose mouths, fat noses, receding chins, charred crepe eyelids, sharp Pera eyes. A shrill pistol-shooting orchestra played to smoking-room seats covered with false Bokharas lit by mosque lamps made from soda bottles; to the Greek major staff; to spurred Anglomaniac palikares, with black hair showing at their gilt-braided cuffs' edges. Half a dozen Russian restaurants to choose from—preferably Restaurant Feodor at the end of the passage in the Grand rue de Pera. On the second floor a low room curdled with smoke, noise, alcohol, into which soupiness the draught from a new arrival cut curious caverns, whereafter the obfuscation again settled at the level of heads, a horizontal partition.

Under this impalpable vault, society was amusing itself—a few English, a few Perotes, but especially Russians. Waitresses sat about at the tables. They fetched the food, gave orders, took them with a gentle distinction; here and there the ease, the fine word, the elegance of some gesture ordinarily servile betrayed their former condition.

A bottle of Greek champagne, which had been shaken en route, drove its cork to the ceiling with a frightful detonation. The chief dish at the next table was an iron box a foot deep, covered with red paper and full of caviar. An officer smothered in ten days' beard wore a commander's insignia pinned to his day coat. He was being entertained by some worn-out, sordid, boresome men, who looked like notaries in flight. A very pretty green Jewess with frizzled head, gold acorns in her ears reaching to her shoulders, put salt into the ice bucket. A woman with her décolleté back to me said in good French: "What'll you have?" She spoke with such authority that I took her for the owner. After I had made up my mind she pulled a tablet from her pocket and scribbled the order herself.

She got up, pushed back her chair and turned:

"Anna Valentinovna: You? Here!"

"Hello. 'Mm. How long've you been in Constantinople?"

"Two hours."

There was no use in her raising her voice on the last two words, she could not sound surprised. She seemed, as usual, to be standing on the steps of the hotel, waiting for me to take her out walking, a cane under her arm, putting on her gloves, kicking the dog out of the way.

"I am a refugee," she said, holding out both hands with a poverty-stricken gesture, "eighteen months on the road, here since last spring. You seem to know your way about. I say, you've got on a good pair of boots. Mine have been resoled in tin and fastened with goose leather. Is Theotocopeuli still in business? I owe him for one hundred and thirty-two pairs."

"But . . . ?"

"No. One doesn't—as Tuchev says—'explain.' You can't understand Russia with the intellect. You can only believe in Russia.

"Still . . . if you want me to talk you'll have to change tables, this one isn't mine. It belongs to the Countess Strakov."

"Marika," this to a young brunette covered with rouge, her neck in a black shirtwaist, "let me steal him. I used to know him in Biarritz, let me present you."

The countess wiped her hand on her apron and extended it. I kissed her hand. She wore a large diamond on her thumb.

We sat. I told Anna how glad I was to see her, that I still loved her, as usual. She accused me of mocking her misfortunes.

"Previous—politely so—sensual, serious, like any other French-man. Passion and safety: Motto for La Ville de Paris at the hour set for adultery. Amiable and annoying, and witty, oh yes, always witty. I haven't been having any for five years, not that sort of fodder," she slapped her arm with a knife-handle.

An English officer wanted his bill. She went over to him, gave it, returned.

"One would think you'd been doing it all your life."

"I am Russian. We are lunatics, we get used to anything, any-where, and, in the end, we beat the bad magicians. We don't clench our fists and stick out our jaws and box with the gods, like the English; we don't *accept,* as you do, any old destiny with grumpy intelligence. It is a bore to wait on a table, but it is just as much a bore to be waited on, and to dance every evening at the Palace Hotel."

"Touching scene, April 1914. Storm on the Virgin's Rock, waves mounting right up to the corner where your mother's room was. How is she?"

"Died of typhus a year ago, in a Turkish hospital, on l'Île des Princes. Thirty-five of my relatives gone. I've lost everything, even my independence and the simple life. I have no fun but my troubles, I reckon they keep me going. Here with the rest, I mean, it's a noise, sad and mad enough possibly, but it lets me empty the days. At the mobilization we went back to Permenikov, our place in Tula, chalk house under a green roof. Agriculture, huntin', chicken-raising, pullets, bandages, reading, nights out on the snow, in the birches, big fires, noise of horses. The revolution changed nothing. The soldiers came back from the front in bunches on the roofs of the trains; those that didn't get scraped off in the tunnels divided the land. It was only in 1918 that things went to pieces. The cloudburst of the revolution, capricious, no system. Although my brother was a Guards officer, we weren't badly treated, mother and I; five versts off Count Samarine (I live with them here) saw his niece buried alive and his nephew torn to pieces with forks, table forks. One morning some deserters and an adjutant wanted to 'enter' Permenikov. I jumped out of bed, hid my pearl necklace in the ashes under the stove, put our rings in the powder puff.

"'Anna Valentinovna, give me all the silver and money, all you've got.' I obeyed. 'Swear by the icons that that is all of it.' I swore. 'Now give me your jewels.' I put the small stuff into his fur cap, bracelets, paste diadems. 'Swear by the icons that that's all there is of it.' I was going to swear, but the adjutant looked at me. I dropped my eyes. 'They're at the pawnshop.' He smiled and let it pass.

"What I wanted was my baby mug, a red one with the Kremlin enameled on it in white over blue, and my little French spoons. I said: 'Leave me my baby mug and my little French spoons.' He gave them back to me and kissed my hand—after taking off my cabochon emerald—and went out politely.

"A month later the place was overrun by stragglers dodging the Czechoslovaks. Wrecked everything. We had to clear in two hours. After that one couldn't get anywhere, everyone was an enemy. There was only one decent half hour and that was when Denikin entered Kiev. Cossacks in parade order, groomed horses shining, distribution of flour, city draped with flags, even the Polish refugees sang; sailors playing accordions, we all thought Russia was delivered. Discipline broke down, disorder, cheating at the rear . . . what the deuce do you expect? That's the way it is in Russia, always."

"And Wrangel?"

"Got no money. My brother is in his army, gets ten thousand rubles a day. You can't live on it. He has no boots and nothing to eat but raw onions. Stefan Bazarov, the officer at that table where I was sitting when you came in, was colonel in the Preobrazhenskys. He's been dishwashing in Yalta. Carved silver cartridge box and topaz-headed dagger, yes, but hasn't a shirt to his name, nothing on under his uniform. We stayed at Odessa until the Bolsheviki arrived. English cruiser took us to l'Île des Princes. I nearly died of typhoid. Nothing left. I have this old silver ruble strung round my neck on a ribbon. Anastasia speaks twelve languages, diploma from the Moscow Institute of Philology, is selling American matches. I haven't slept between sheets for two years."

She said all this in a tone plaintive but conventional, no painful memory seemed to be attached to the words. At times she seemed rather to exult in having paid off some sort of mystical debt to Providence.

The orchestra played "Fi-Fi." Half submerged, half drowning in the harmony, the first violin rose now and then from the other sounds.

"You got a royal flush and won't bet on it."

The toothless gamblers slammed down their cards like hatchets.

Anna brought a basket of fruit and stood before me. Eating the grapes, she continued:

"It all sounds like pitching a tale, romantic, yes, Russia is romantic or whatever . . . pleasure, boredom. All of it magnetism. The women add to it, they are mixed up in everything, war, politics, espionage, business. They ride on the generals' private trains, they walk into the government offices, they are in forests, in the prisons, on the rivers, and they don't come in like the French women to bring more common sense and economy. Wherever we are, things always go to extremes. Look at Constantinople, poverty is incredible, squandering, worse than ever, crazy, drink, cheating, priggishness, people die and they do business with a cleverness and a dishonesty that make even Pera sit up."

I tried to divert her by prophesying a change.

"Yes," she said, without alteration of tone, "we *may* go back to Russia, some day, *per—haps* . . ."

This last word took on an intonation, silky distant. It laid no burden on the future, it merely underlined it, as if by a stroke light as the blue pines and the horizon, a mirage which made no one its dupe. Even concrete statements undergo this curious transformation upon the lips of the Russians, they become like a shadow of verity, they lose all their motive and force. One began to think that all she had just been saying had come out of the nonexistent; annulling the speech and the grammar; instead of bringing words to the actual, it seemed merely to set them free of their meaning, to let them drift further and still further from the real. They alluded to the past, then to a past more distant, till even yesterday assumed the odor of legend.

"*Per—haps* . . ."

As she had said it on the Adour, her hair flying in the wind, driving her hundred H.P. Fiat, breakneck (à tombeau ouvert) like a troika. She had been engaged to Vladimir Yermolov; she didn't care for him much, but he sent her poems written in blood, really his own blood. I asked her to marry me. She said, "We shall see. All things are possible, since they carry in themselves the seeds of their contraries."

I found her just as she had been, attended by a charm which entoiled one, but which ended a few paces from her. One looked into her eyes as into a bath; they were the color of water in which the swimmer can see the river bottom at a hundred yards from the bank. I would have left everything to follow her, and then the war came between us.

"I'm married, you know, got children . . ."

I saw a slight cloud in her eyes, for a moment, like the shift of light on submarine foliage or against the flaw of an emerald. She turned her head away, as Orientals will when you look at them.

"You don't look like a père de famille. You'll have that baby face all your life . . . You see I was right . . . you didn't need me after all."

"Alas! my heart is as full of notches as a conscript's knife-handle a month before his discharge. What can I do for you, Anna?"

"Nothing. I am making enough to get my opera cloak out of hock. Then I shall have enough to get to Paris on the cheap, on the train, that's cheaper than the boat fare. We all want to get to Paris."

"Let me, for God's sake, get you the ticket."

"I've got the money for the ticket. Old Samarine pawned it on the quiet, wanted the money for drink. I've got three one-thousand-franc City of Paris bonds sewn up in the lining; naturally I don't want to talk about it with the police."

"I think we'd better go get it out."

I looked at my watch. The shop was open till twelve—open, that is, until the last boat . . . People wanted to hock something to get a bed for the night, one hundred francs.

The high commissioner's curfew was at one. Anna got permission to leave the restaurant. The orchestra was playing tunes gradually more plaintive and delicate, like a troop of singers going off into the distance. Everyone joined in the chorus. The tables were in disorder, cigarette ashes, the long cardboard cigarette butts, Angora cats prowling from table to table, electric fans stirring the fetid air, piano out of key, all this mess obliterated by the grave singing voices of the Russians, going up to the low ceiling like a prayer of exile.

"Russia can never die." Anna said this as we passed out. "Misery makes a new soul. Our youth is gone, ruined, but the next lot, Russians in Constantinople, in Baku, in Vladivostok, in Sakhalin, all a love of Russia, intenser. Today it needs little time to make a great empire, even less to destroy one. The bottom of the wheel is up tomorrow. Don't forget that in Paris . . . at bottom, no. I don't really believe it. Everything will die, it has to for resurrection."

We had to go to her lodgings for the pawn ticket and her passport. She lived in a slum by the docks. The wind from the Black Sea swept in over the Bosphorus. Along the Petits Champs, Italian carabinieri, French gendarmes, military police in red caps, were apparently on the lookout for an international criminal; each corner his deathtrap. The smell of rouge, pomades, greasy hair roots, invited one into the Bar de la Belle Crète. Tramcars like great red-and-gold lacquer boxes rushed creaking by one. British Admiralty wireless crackled over the station by the old Genoese tower.

"Who'd have thought before dinner we should be here together?" I said. "I have thought of you . . . often . . . I knew we'd meet again sometime."

"I didn't."

We went on over ill-paved streets clogged with litter, past Greek cabarets with the Allied flags painted on the windowpanes, with portraits of Venizelos in farm costume and black-rimmed spectacles over the doors. Turks were taking their coffee on the sidewalks in spite of the wind, sitting on old sofas with their stuffings leaking out. Under the frozen light, a cinema poster showed an auto at full tilt with a woman tied into it, changing the gear with her teeth. There were signs: "This street closed to French troops"; an orchestrophone sputtered; a dromedary loaded with carrots and cabbages, like a hairy bridge, blocked the path with spread legs. Turkish houses of satin-gray sycamore wood stuck their broken roofs into the reddish sky. We went down a slope into a cellar where three people were having supper. They had been the three largest proprietors in Tula, Prince Samarine and his two sisters, Georgina and Anika, Anna's cousins. The place smelt of alcohol and phosphorus, mixed with that stalish Russian odor of faded cashmere and leather. The old women, dames d'honneur to the empress mother, wore the yellow ribbons of the Order of Catherine pinned to their shirtwaists. They were breeding rabbits under the bed, they prayed to their icons bobbing their old pates, which the English had shaved at Lemnos to get rid of the lice: they were eating from broken crockery with old family silver saved from the wreckage, their pale faces lit by the one candle that guttered in a bottle neck; faces brutalized by their adventures.

One of them kept saying: "I want to go back to Russia." And the other, "You can't go back, they'll cut your throat," and with the antiphony, she stretched her crossed wrists in front of her and moved her hands inward like scissor blades, grinning.

Prince Samarine offered me a chair with an elaborate politeness. He looked like a St. Nicholas mobilized in a long English artillery coat, with a full-size Légion d'honneur in his buttonhole.

"Thank you, sir. You will take tea with us? I am sorry I have no real brandy to offer you, *Napoleon the First*."

On the death of Emperor Alexander he had left court; and married a rich religious crank. A little later he had pretended to get religious, proposed that they should both abandon the world, each leaving their fortune to the other. She bit. When the doors of her nunnery had firmly closed behind her he emerged from the monastery where he had been very careful not to take vows. He got the courts to turn over the property to him and then went to Paris, where he had passed twenty-eight years amusing himself, after which he returned to Tula dead broke and lived en villégiature on his sisters.

"And Paris is still as, as 'pschutt,' as, as 'vlan' as it ever was? Do they still use the expression? I hear the Jews set the fashion. Look what they've brought us to. By God, I resigned from the Jockey Club the day they elected Baron Gustave. I tell you. Those were the days."

The Alexander II samovar with the Samarine blazon bubbled.

"They were days! Decorative Arts lottery, Molier's Circus. Fifine winning at Auteuil, June 5th, 1886. Princesse de Sagan's animal ball. I went as a white rat, and M. de Germiny was priceless as an orang. He was priceless. He exhibited me as 'Half beaver, a bad hat, fur de luxe.' I tell you, he was awfully clever."

Anna started to go. The old boy held me by my coat button, puffing his rummy breath into my face.

"Thank you, sir, it mustn't be said that the Samarines let you go off like this. You must come see us at Kolovskaya, our own place. We'll be getting back there before long now. I've got a bit of Tokay; Franz Joseph, the emperor, gave it me, and partridge shooting. Chinese partridges, Semmering pheasants, and deer brought up on human milk."

"I want to go back to Russia." The old woman, excited by this reminiscence, began again. "You can't, Georgina, they'll cut your throat." The other again made the scissor gesture. "I want to go back to Russia . . ." It continued.

We went back toward Pera, Anna holding my arm, her face showing pale under every lamppost, under her oilcloth hat, with her reddish hair sticking out in bunches about it; thin in her knitted jumper hidden beneath a dust coat.

Indifference—I don't know—or a wish not to appeal for pity kept in her distress. Or perhaps this tonelessness, this lack of response or resonance came from the abuse of nerves, the long drawn-out series of horrors she had seen about her. I wanted to give myself to her, to put off my departure, to reconcile her with her destiny. I don't know. She seemed not to want it. She seemed not to want to soften her destiny. Anything I could say only came up against a sort of secret urge, always firmer.

Street hawkers passed, carrying lighted baskets full of grapes with a candle in the middle showing through them. As we came to Le Tunnel people were streaming in from the street. "Russian Press Bureau . . . there's Wrangel's map."

A row of tin electrics showed a map of Russia, cut by a thread which passed through Elisavetgrad, Lozovaya, Slavyansk, outlining [the] Crimea, the wheat ports, the beginnings of the Black Country, the mines.

"We must keep a stiff lip, mustn't abandon Wrangel. All these people, all living on hope."

"You say 'hope' and you aren't 'having any' yourself."

An imperceptible sigh.

"Done with it."

The Russians, in clumps, gossiping over the telegrams, announcements of boat arrivals from [the] Crimea. All leaning over the edge of that abyss, Red Russia, out of which comes nothing but cries, gunshots, whipcracks, never any news of one's relatives, shut in there, hopeless. In the slow-coming darkness they loitered, nothing to do, gregarious and nocturnal, odd costumes and disguises, unbelievable. Intelligentsia, their hair plastered down with bear's grease, in Turkish slippers, talking bad logic, glowering through black iron-rimmed spectacles. Ambiguous Slavic rabble, sexless, ageless, one in high heels, gray suit patched at the knees, followed by a priceless King Charles spaniel, jabbering with the voices of coachmen. Uniforms (by courtesy), lancers in duck-hunting blouses, infantry with regimental badges sewed on to the velvet collars of evening suits. A quartermaster general in a bicycle suit, with the cross and full collar of St. Anne, giving his arm to his poor old mother; a colonel of transport trains in a silk muffler, selling the *Gazette de Sebastopol*. And nearly all with that Oriental expression which shows nothing, neither boredom nor impatience, nor sadness—nothing but immense fatigue.

Near the Press Bureau we stopped by a side alley under the sign "Polack's Oriental Stores, Salon de Mode, Great choice of objects de luxe exported from Russia." We slid under the half-closed iron blind. Behind a counter red-eyed, towheaded Polack and his sons were taking an inventory by the light of a kerosene lamp. One checking the day's loans on silver, pictures, lace, carpets, underwear, evening frocks; flimsy pink satins, hanging rumpled in the shadows. Furs at the further end, hanging from pegs, a sort of gigantic "Return from the Hunt"; ermines gone yellow, sables worn and rusty, and the men's coats especially, heavy beyond anything we know in the West.

Anna finally got her beaver fur. The lining intact. The Paris bonds were still there.

A mist came over her eyes.

"Thank you, but I can't bear owing it to you."

"Come, buck up, Anna. After all I have friends in Paris; you might even tell my wife, and discuss me, as they usually do in Russian novels, à la Sologub or Chekhov."

"I will go to Paris, *for me*. That will be the coda of the concerto. Mind you I'm not going back *there,* not ever." She pointed over the Golden Horn, over past the Bosphorus and the sea, the route she had come by.

"I will not see the old place, not again. I wouldn't, not if I could. The old life is gone, gone. There is nothing left of it. I am young, not really, I know what I'm saying. You are going on further east, you are my friend, so I can tell you frankly; it's finished. At Paris I shall go to the Hotel Voltaire, because the Louvre is royal at five in the afternoon in October; I shall put the family affairs in order, I shall look into the church in the rue Pierre le Grand, where I was baptized. I shall be about broke in two weeks. Then I shall finish it, I know too much. I hope you will think of me . . . as I think of you."

She said good-bye to me gently. And I saw nothing but a vague form moving from me indistinctly in the darkness.

The Roman Night

ᴇᴈ Cats warbled in the hotel garden. A barking dog drove them out and returned with tongue lolling and blue from eating black-berries or fountain pens. While they were chucking the trunks upside down onto a hotel bus, Isabel's mother waited in the hall, a small woman, excessively preserved by milk of cucumbers and egoism, her wrinkles were stitched in behind her ears, her bosom larded with an imitation pearl necklace whereof the sea-born original reposed in her small tightly gripped crocodile handbag.

When she saw me, she squealed:

"I give my daughter into your charge. Isabel don't want to go back to France with me. I can't do anything with her. She is aerial. She don't care about anything. You are an educated, rea-sonable man, do look after her. Did you want her? She isn't here. She's gone off God knows where, without her maid. She has taken bottles, a blanket, and a spade-cane to kill lizards, she said she was without hope and that my hypocrisy was a nuisance. Those young people drink like a drain, and stuff without any label. She does nothing she doesn't like—takes her life like a dream. Things that amused us, the four-step, Hungarian lace, jackstraws, Vene-tian painting, are no longer in fashion. The world sheds its skin once in every thirty years. At your age, I said to her, I had five children already. She said: It must have ruined your figure. She don't care about clothes. She won't go out in society. My feelings and prejudices tickle her to death. She compels herself to enjoy everything—out of irony. She knows nothing. She has no artistic taste. What she writes is all rubbish. Morally, you might say, she has melted, she is open to anything, she congratulates herself when it happens or ridicules it; she says she is under a curse, and then laughs. I'll probably miss my train. The truth is the worm has got into the fruit. What is this lunacy? Tell me."

"It's the sacrificed generation, ma'am. The men have gone off to be soldiers, and the women have all gone crazy. Destiny only has piled on catastrophes. In fact Isabel is a victim of this contra-snobbism to which a delicate soul finally clings. Sooner or later, one can't meet people unless one knows there is no personal reason for doing it."

She had the motor stopped because it prevented her being heard:

". . . take note until she was fifteen there wasn't a better brought up child," at this point, she handed me the key of her room, which she had forgotten to give to the porter. —I also forgot it until the heavy brass triangular label wore a hole in my pocket, wherethrough it attained the street.

*

* *

Professor Ovide's GRAPHOLOGICAL STUDIES.

Study No. 34. Isabel.

Writing of a young woman with delicate somewhat mobile face. Constitution sanguine. Although she lives in comfort it is doubtful whether she belongs by birth to an aristocratic circle of acquaintance. Intelligence superficial but sufficient to please. She has personal ideas, but they are not always logical. A difficult temper.

More of a coquette than she would wish to confess, she has a certain moderation and dislikes anything coarse. She has more independence than pride and may even be deficient in this latter.

Expansive and amiable in company. Her sincerity is open to question. Her heart is rather dry but is capable of melting at moments. She needs to rule and influence the people she loves. The sensuality which forms part of her character is not over-refined.

I reread this graphological study of Isabel obtained from Professor Ovide of St. Maur-les-Fossés in the beginning of our acquaintance. I had used it to know her better and had had it long enough to find out that the diagnosis was false. Only a few approximate shots in the playful soul reader's jargon resisted experimental demonstration, and these amused her more quickly than they did anyone else.

Isabel was of an impulsive secretive nature. I had no time to learn this or in general to make her acquaintance until after we had shared those delights which used, in time past, to crown and cement the affections. The evening of our first meeting at the Valle Theatre she said that I looked like a sycamore. We settled the matter, there, in the carriage which was taking her home to her mother. The rules of the game were very much simplified. Passion lost thus its graduated interest, but the laws of exchanges, sentimental, magnetic, and chemical, had more play and gained a certain verity or exactitude.

Isabel confessed to me, shortly after, that she never lost an opportunity of making this spontaneous gift of her favors; she was impelled perhaps by an excess of modesty, to which she sacrificed her virtue without hesitation. She did this affably in the belief that it would be to the profit of her intelligence and sensibility. The intelligence was mediocre, and I doubt whether the sensibility had ever perverted this heart "rather dry but capable of melting at moments," as indicated for me by Professor Ovide.

Nevertheless we found ourselves solidly in the midst of a confident intimacy, such as is rarely the privilege of unprejudiced people. By a curious retrogression, occasioned doubtless by the manner of our becoming acquainted—seeing that you can't but pay for upsetting any natural order—I had very soon felt for Isabel the whole gamut of sentiments—in reverse order—beginning with indifference and fatigue, continuing into tenderness; from pleasure moving to love, and thence into curiosity and entertainment.

We saw each other very often. Isabel spent long months in Rome without my being ever able to find a sole reason for her staying in that dreary unpicturesque city.

When I asked if she intended to die there, she said:

"Possibly; at any rate you endeavor to conquer habit, that chain spitting monster, with his swinging pendulum of a tail."

Her pension looked out on the old fortifications near Porta Pia. My life was focused on a courtyard, from the second floor of the Palazzo Farnese, for I was a pupil of the École de Rome. I had a card file full of notes, a ladder for getting down books from the upper shelves, a clotty inkwell. At six o'clock I went to the corner room to say good-bye to dear teacher. He read decadent African authors, sitting in a crimson velvet armchair, surrounded by Angoras and pumice-colored cats, like those about Trajan's Column. I have not forgotten the spectacles set like two fat iceflakes on his forehead, his white hair cantankerous as the nature beneath it, the head like that of a peasant Erasmus, a dark shadow outlined against the milky Janiculum. I went out through draughty corridors. The doorkeeper wafted me a smile impeded by his silver braidings.

Isabel waited by the Tiber. We walked back toward the higher parts of the town. Her figure was notable in that country of long-busted and short-thighed women. She had a minute head "full of water," as she said in excusing her eccentricities. Had she ever been capable of a body? Beneath the shoulders she divided instantly into legs, thin, pointed like those of a compass, with which she pinpricked the paving. On her right ankle she wore a heavy African slave ring of carved copper, which made her limp as she walked.

Willingly, before a third person, she kept her mouth shut, but tête-à-tête she let out anything that came into her head. She did not like acquaintances, especially those which one can make in hotels and pensions—which dislike is an error.

I warned her against asceticism. She replied:

"Real ascetics are people who love society, Mother for example. Vice, virtue? Society takes the place of them, and of everything else." Isabel hated her mother and lost no chance of poking fun at her—never said a decent thing about her except behind her back. At table she seemed to watch her moment for leaping on her.

Isabel wrinkled her eyes in smiling and chewed a little ivory cigarette holder to keep from biting her nails. As if to put her interlocutor in the presence of a completed idea, and to invite him to reply to it, she stretched out her open hands in ending a sentence. The palms were a vivid pink.

She had no brains in general, though like all women she seemed to in her letters. The scraps of diary which she showed me appeared to be without interest. But she spat blood, cheated me at poker, and had a love of deception in contrast with her physical courage.

I had seen her in accidents bandaging others, and forgetting to have herself bandaged. During thirty-six months of the war she drove a surgical auto near Noyon.

In her room, Isabel ordered drinks, would stop halfway through a glass, her eyes filling with tears as if the liquor had opened some mysterious, sensitive threshold; then she would finish it. She sat cross-legged on the floor, drawing her feet up under her, her bony knees creaking with dry arthritis, smoking like an indolent feline. She remained thus for hours, inactive, cynical, genital.

In spring Isabel made acquaintances, having lived alone all the winter.

"What do you think of Igor?"

I grumbled about his beauty, his venomous eyes, the bluster of colored posters: Igor, large cinematograph star, in dress suit, on the desert strand, the poor student, in antechambers hung with brocade; his irritating profile rose amid roofs; his sallow skin punctuated with sparks, his pale cream-soaked hands among those of wagoners handling stacked cards in the dives.

"He's like a maple," said Isabel.

Igor is Graeco-Irish. His father is a general in the Greek army and his mother a general of the Irish rebels. The first time I met him at Isabel's, she sighed, she looked at the two of us:

"Life is a tissue of contrasts."

It was the time when Isabel was taking vulnerary, she surrounded herself with prismatic crystals; breakfasted on ginger; bought a Florentine cupboard-bed; received a magnolia flower each morning from an unknown hand; gave strange commissions to the servants; couldn't touch buckskin without fainting. She separated herself from life by faked arguments; she received me on panther skins; her speech grew elliptical. I complained that she went to no parties.

"Yes, but I go out every night."

"?"

"In the sleep world."

One day she took me into her room. Above the bed were pinned bills, letters, photos of men doing the hundred-yard dash, and a notice saying: Don't forget to love Igor on Saturday. I thought it was not my place to ask questions. But she looked at me.

"Your eye grows dull," she said: "Igor has eyes of crystal. I do not love the heroes of resignation."

"Me, I like women who make their own hats, and who suffer disappointment."

"As you like. But be on your guard against *métrites*."

She put down her glass on a gramophone disk and watched it revolve to the tune of:

> Naples! Naples! I would die
> 'Neath your enchanting sky.

"You . . ."

"Don't speak," she interrupted. "I feel that you are going to say: Keep me, you'll see, I bring luck."

Igor had a friend, Wanda, to whom Isabel introduced me: she was Polish, believed in ghosts. We made nocturnal excursions to the Ostian shore. I sat on the strapontin. Isabel had Wanda to right of her and Igor to left of her, she held their similar hands. Her sincerity was disconcerting. To keep from abusing her I buffooned:

"I would rather be first in my village than second in Rome, or third . . ."

Under cover of informality and insolence I unveiled my lost and refound difficulties. I would have lived near Isabel, loving her perfectly as one does things at a distance. But at evening I was surprised to find myself enjoying the qualities in her which I couldn't but detest in the morning, her imprudences, her opaque soul and transparent robes, the promptitude and low quality of her favors.

From Wanda Isabel learned the smell of red hair, the reason why she was sad after lunch, the best shops for silk jerseys, unknown Levantine card combinations based on astrology; she learned to kill bees and suck out their honey. It was the reign of lemons and grapefruit, of jujubes and tricolored bonbons. Isabel painted her trunks in lozenges and in spirals, sought emblems, sent anonymous letters to politicians, bought mosaic brooches, wore chasubles, disturbed the neighborhood by nocturnal clamor, preached poverty, discovered a lesion in her aorta.

I was, during this period, less unhappy. Isabel summoned me to public gardens. On their benches she confided that she would commit suicide by inhaling gas, that she didn't want to be carried into a pharmacy.

Her thought hesitated, like a bat in the daylight.

Ludicrous and pale, she repeated:

"I have come to a crossroads . . ."

To console her I recited the quatrain of Max, the good La Fontaine of rue Ravignan:

> Hercules in childhood, setting out
> found two ways before him
> One led to vice and one to virtue
> Had he continued the first he would have
> found without doubt
> Some very confusing bifurcations.

I met Wanda one morning in the Piazza Sant' Isidro. They had just dug up a temple of Jupiter in making the cellar for a new branch of the Banca Commerciale. Photographers were working for the illustrated papers. It was an opportunity for a walk. It was raining. Wanda, all pink and mauve, was lodged in an unsinkable oilskin.

I scolded her for her spirit of domination, her clever fencing, her gentle and evil habits, in short for the ambuscade Isabel had got herself into.

"You don't know how I met Isabel? I'm red-headed, but she's the one who is jealous. She waited all night on Igor's doorstep. Then I came out. She didn't know me, but she began it.

"She said, 'I've got something to say to you.' I took her home with me. She stayed there . . .

"It was more than a week before we dared to own up to Igor."

The subcellars of the bank were fenced in by plaques of reed matting amid which the recently discovered two-fronted Jupiter rose frigid and dominating, the first president of the company.

114

"You don't like my story?"

"I shudder at the disorder and unproductivity of all you contemporary females. Sexual functionaries."

"What do you mean . . . keep it up, grumble . . . can't you see that all these goings on of Isabel's are only mortifications intended to humble her pride?"

"You are a gentle sophism. That's all there is to you," I said, turning to leave her.

She called me back:

"Say, do you think that I'm like a scarlet oak, really?"

Isabel then dug up a mulatto. His name was Jack, he kept up his pants with a nickel-plated belt. With heel and toe of his patent leather pumps he engraved magic indecipherable abracadabra on polished floors. His nails like rosy dewdrops at his fingertips. He touched the floor with his crinkly hair effortlessly, back or front. He was a fetishist and adored ladies' handbags. They were seen together on the Palatine and in the Excelsior Bar.

Isabel was about to describe him, but I anticipated her:

"Don't tell me that he is like a wild-rose tree."

She spent the days writing his name on bits of paper, which she rolled up into pellets and swallowed.

Soon she preferred denatured alcohol, plug tobacco, jigs in galoshes, the noisiest fanfares, silver gilt tableware, pants in gooseberry-colored satin, capes made of samples sewn, end on, to each other.

"Jack loves me," said Isabel. "He asks me for letters and photographs. His skin is speckled like porcelain. He has prehensile feet and he can climb down a tree headfirst like a cat. He is enormous . . . as Buffon says of the elephant, a monster in matter. He can forge signatures and pick locks. When he comes to see me he says: 'I can't go 'way without a souvenir'."

She added:

"I love him. He talks so nicely, nasty words, don't you know, but he makes them sound nice. We were like magnetic poles from the first. He takes away my headaches, with his big dark hands on my forehead; who are you to despise me for it? And Mother says I'm intractable. A change of love works on me like a change of climate on other people."

When did Isabel see him? One never met him about. But we received anonymous envelopes containing monstrous photographs of our friend. Examining them more closely we found that her head had been cut off and pasted on. I discovered a bracelet I had given her in a second-hand dealer's in the Trastevere.

Wanda said to me:

"Yesterday morning when I was dressing, someone rang the bell. I didn't open the door as I was alone. I asked who was there. A man mumbled, 'Let me come in, I'm a friend.' I did not. He went off down the stairs. That was all."

Things being in this condition, Isabel, as I have said, disappeared at the moment of her mother's departure from the Immortal City. I waited, knowing she would make a sign fairly soon. But she didn't. Her absence was, at times, pleasing; more often it was painful: we cease to care about mystery when our friends become lovers of cryptograms. My fears increased. After a day without her my room offered me but chilly reception. I lived on impatiences, deploring life's poor technique, hurrying up to chance crowds in the street, reacting to newspaper headlines; I was a savant, I couldn't get used to living—as one should in these days—without documentation, without preliminary inquiries, compounding daily with madness.

One evening I found Igor and Wanda in front of a café. They were imbibing saffron-colored drinks beneath the petrified flounces of the Church of Jesus.

Isabel had given no sign of life to any of us.

"All I know is from the masseuse," said Wanda. "She's rented a house outside the walls, Pavilion No. 12 in a Boche villa that's got the name of a brewery. It's further than the Porta del Popolo, a hole in between two hills, in a damp garden smothered in shadow . . ."

Igor interrupted her:

"The owner has come out of a German fairy tale, with a knitted wool cap and a lot of bats in his beard? He lives in the central châlet with bloodhounds that sniff under the door? That's the one. I know it 'cause we once did a film there."

"Let's go down to supper with her," I said. "Surprise party."

We loaded champagne into a cab, with a basket of fruit and a kilo of ice to cool the drinks.

The horse had to stop halfway up.

We took out the provisions. Igor and Wanda giggled in the darkness, imitating the noises of a stable, or noisily kissing the backs of their hands.

The yowling of dogs shook the night. We groped our way under the overarched fig trees. Then the alley twisted and stopped before a wall of bamboos, the leaves rustled. We were in mid-jungle, the lion in the Borghese Gardens zoo added to the illusion by roaring.

At a white pavilion marked No. 12 Wanda knocked, gently. Then loudly. We called. A field mouse fled. We stood grouped, silent, dazzled by the darkness, our arms loaded with bottles, the ice scorching my fingers.

Igor proposed to get in from the other side of the garden. We climbed the wall by the aid of a pine tree whose cones fell with a clatter. No noise, no light from inside. I struck a match, which lit up part of the porch. The door was open. I turned the electric button. A central lamp hanging on its wire glared at us and filled the room with bleak light. We tasted a musky odor. Igor set down the champagne and went forward: in the bedroom Isabel lay on the floor, naked, immobile, with black marks on her throat.

The Six-Day Night

~§ For three evenings one had seen her. She was alone save during the dances, all of which she danced with the instructor or with one of the other girls. When anyone asked her she refused, me as well as anyone else, although I had come for her, and she knew it. It wasn't her milky back, her jet dress with its shimmering rain of sequins, or the excess of onyx jewelry, which included her own eyes, their brows blackened and stretched back in wire-thick bands meeting her ear lobes, it was rather her flattened nose, the heaving of her bosom, her fine Jewish complexion, somewhat like a sulphated vine, her ambiguous isolation, and also the curious maneuvers which she executed several times an evening toward the lavabo and the telephone.

She did not let the headwaiter pay for her drinks. She went from short ones to long ones. On the third evening between midnight and two a.m. she put away two bottles of champagne, six anisettes, and a quarter decanter of brandy, not forgetting the toothpicks and green almonds.

She went up to the telephone; me behind her. "It's Leah. Got good milk? Goin' all right? No stitch in his side? Has he eaten? Eh? From the baby bottle?"

We got better acquainted in the waterless lavatory littered with petals, straws, broken dolls, cocaine, rendezvoux, and poudre Rachel. She looked at herself pitilessly under the lamp, until her lips met their reflection in the mirror. I drew a heart on the misted surface. She shrugged one shoulder.

The silver Chinese officials on her blouse consulted at the entrance of a pagoda.

"Nothing to let?" I asked, placing a finger on the pagoda doorway each time this part of the design was repeated on her bosom. She pulled herself up like a ramrod.

"Say, are you taken often like this?"

The female attendant, who was drying her hands on an overcoat, turned round and interceded for me.

"Yes, you look like a gentleman," said Leah, "but I always go wrong when I'm jagged."

Sprouting breast high from the lifted violin bows in the balcony we saw Negroes dressed for the beach, chewing emptiness, shaking with consecrated paludism. Twisted copper iris, Metro saplings, lit up landscapes of a Seine no longer disfigured with factories, but inundated with poesy and with grinning shivering nudes washing up. Dancers, glued together, clicked their heels in the waltzing basin. The room smelt of beef tea, addled eggs, armpits, and the perfume Un Jour Viendra.

"Where do you live," I said to her, "I love you."

"You kiddin' or do you mean it?"

"Both. I always am, do."

She, unavoidably.

"I think I've seen you, somewhere."

"You are my sister," I said, kissing her dress, "and indispensable."

I must have seemed fresh, contemptible, and void of free will. She shook herself free.

"You seem to be in an awful hurry."

"No, but I do everything that I do quickly and badly, for fear I'll stop wanting to before I finish."

"It's nearly two. I got to beat it."

"Not till you tell me why you disappear every two minutes. Have you *got any*?"

She opened her eyes like a pair of poached eggs.

"Coco? Not likely. I don't want to get five years."

"Well?"

"It's for news of my friend, he's working."

"What at?"

"He's a stayer, a six-day man. He's riding in a six-day race. What! Never heard of Pettimatheu, where you come from?"

And she wrapped herself up in ninety-eight white rabbits.

"Can't keep my coachman up nights. Get me a taxi; one that'll go to Grenelle."

Along the curves of the Seine the meter clicked like a lunatic heart. Pink unstrung pearls along the Cours-la-Reine, phosphorescent drains, her dry cough, attempted effusions, swearing to myself to put an end to ambiguities, and—after the Champ-de-Mars, wagonloads of blue cabbages.

"I like fiacres," I said, "we ought to take a fiacre and live in it for a month or so, until we knew its lamps and springs and tires. To think that the blinds in the Urbaines only pull down halfway, and how nice it is to 'fall on a calf' that isn't too hot, when Paris moves in the mist and we head for depopulation."

Grenelle. The water bends under the yoke of the bridge. There are red flares on the lover's parapet, green ones for business men, 14 f. 25.

Me, nervously:

"You live in Paris?"

"G' 'an! Who's talkin' about where I live. I'm goin' to the Vel' d'hiv [Winter Velodrome] for the two o'clock prizes."

*

* *

A subterranean passage led to the swell seats. Carpets from La Place Clichy blown off the floor by the drafts. Halfway through, there was a thunder over our heads. The laths groaned. Then we came to the wooden arena with its glass roof containing a fog split by luminous conic sections. From beneath their enameled umbrellas the voltaic lamps watched the track; Leah rose to her tiptoes commandingly.

"You see, yellow and black . . . the wasps. That's the ace team. It's Van den Hoven riding. They'll wake up Pettimatheu for the two o'clock heat."

Shrill whistles pierced the air. There were four thousand yells, Parisian yells, coming from well down in the throat.

The Australian tried to weed 'em out. The sprints began. Above the advertising signs, I saw the tense gazes and burning eyes of the "cheap seats." The orchestra blared. Latriche was singing. They took up the chorus of "Hardi Coco," thus increasing the pace. The sixteen racers repassed unfailingly every twenty seconds in a compact platoon. The swell seats were at the back of the velodrome. The curves at each end of it rose like walls which the runners climbed at each lap, up to the petrol ad.

LA PLUS HOMOGÈNE DES ESSENCES.

The scoreboard was in action. Numbers came down. Others showed there.

4th NIGHT.   85th hour, 2,300 kilometers 650.

"Heh. There he is. That's my boy getting on," said Leah.

Pettimatheu still moved about by himself, stretching, his hair frizzled, his neck dirty, his eyes tricky as a cat's.

"He's a corker for the fourth night, that kid is."

The nickeled megaphone announced two 100-franc bonuses, emphasized by some pistol shots.

"Come on. The pace'll get stiffer. There. He sees us."

He had seen me. I was holding Leah's hand. We exchanged male hostile glances.

Now drawn out into file, the sound of each lap was briefer than the preceding, and at the bell the sixteen men passed, like roulette balls projected in straight lines from the twisted curve-banking.

"Leah," I murmured, "I'd like to be what that old Calvinist Agrippa d'Aubigné calls 'cradled in delights.' What do you take in the morning?"

The crowd yowled inhumanly.

"Nah," she said, "you're barmy. Not while the boy's there on the wood, I couldn't look myself in the face, I'd think meself dirt while that kid's there for six days and nights. I couldn't think of anything but 'im."

They set off on the heat like carp after a hunk of bread, the woolly Italian, the Swiss giant, the Corsican noncoms, and all the Negroes and blond-headed Flemings.

"It's over, the Australian's got it. The dirty old tarbelly. Pettimatheu's got hisself boxed. He's going to get off. Let's go see the old dear."

The racers' quarters were stuck up at one end of the track, at the smaller turn. Each man had a plank cell, with a camp bed shut off by curtains. The stencil: VELOX STAND, team PETTI-MATHEU-VAN DEN HOVEN. A reflector threw light into the depths of the cabins, so that the crowd lost none of their favorites' movements, even while the latter were asleep. The rubbers-down came and went in white hospital blouses, with a noise of plates, among the spots of petrol and graphite, mixing embrocations on the garden chairs out of eggs and camphor. Loose ball bearings, frames, rubber washers, black cotton swabs swimming in basins. Pettimatheu was stretched on his back, his hands behind his nape, delivering his hairy, strong-veined thighs to the masseur, who pummeled them till they were soft as a cloth.

"Bibby, let me kiss him," said Leah to the manager.

Pettimatheu opened one eye.

"That's all right," he said, crossly, pushing her away, "let him get on with his job."

"You ain't shaved, you ruffian."

"Shut up."

There was a silence. The squad passed, strung out, brushing by us, their shadows thrown on the tents. Naked legs moved like machines, Van den Hoven yelled as he passed us.

"Speed her up tomorrow."

I was introduced to Pettimatheu, but he couldn't seem to see me. He snorted. It'd teach him to hurry himself for a bloody whore of a prize. A dirty hundred francs. Bloody public. Tight-wads! Whoremasters, and their skirts with 'em, when they ain't got some other fellow's.

His thighs were now like moist ivory.

"Get up, you there, Pettimatheu," yelled the inexorable cheap seats from above the Peugeot lions. But he made a sign that he was fed up.

Stained mechanics in khaki shirts, with five days' beard, wound the handlebars with tarred thread, stacked up the wheels that needed going over, tightened a nut here and there.

Pettimatheu wasn't happy.

"Me stomach, when in hell are you going to get round to me stomach."

The masseur pulled away the elastic breeches-band, over the navel one spied, "4th regiment of Zouaves, 1st company," and the motto "To the uttermost"; he passed the flat of his hand over the cyclist's intestines.

"Put some talcum on me backside."

The men who had been replaced got off their machines for two hours' sleep. Their managers stopped them, catching the saddles and handlebars, unwrapped their straps from the pedals, and conducted their colts with tender care to their couches.

Then everything quieted down for the night; in spite of the noise, the contestants snored. Others sitting up in their coverlets joked from one bed to another as in barracks. One heard the puffing of bicycle pumps followed by the noise of air escaping the valves.

Pettimatheu lay consistently on his back, his fingers adorned with square black-rimmed nails and large aluminum rings, his hands crossed on his breast. Leah sat at his feet daubing on rouge. I removed myself.

Behind the shack I could hear Pettimatheu.

"Didn't ah tell yuh teh keep outer Maxims, while ah'm racin'?"

Leah explained that she was too nervous, that she couldn't stay in her room. She couldn't sleep. She thought only of him, of his lovely legs pushin' it along, of his lovely face with his black curly hair and his Charlie mustache, and his firm chin, his eyes on the tire back of the pacemaker, his crimson sweater with pearl buttons on the shoulder. Was it the first time? Hadn't she lived at the end of a telegraph wire all the time he was racing last year in Madison Square Garden?

Crushed by the 105 hours of labor and the 2,872 kil. 580, the riders strung out in single file, to the silvery sound of ball bearings. A Negro was in the lead. Some had put on goggles. Sometimes a tire would burst or a chain break. They would rush his mate out of bed and plank him on the saddle; and, still asleep, he would stick to the skein of racers. The round grew monotonous, as usual at ends of night, where save from absolute giving out no one thinks of leaving. A ten-ton silence descended.

Leah joined me in the grandstand.

"Beat it. He can't sleep with you here. He's watching us all the time. He goes barmy to think I'm with someone and he can't leave his shack. The more tired he gets the more he's nervous.

"It ain't that he dislikes you, he says you're all right, only about half-siphon," she went on. "It's me he's annoyed with. He don't want me to go to Maxim's or dance. He's a regular cave man."

I learned thus that Pettimatheu allowed her to go only to the Excelsior, a racers' brasserie, for her letters and visits. There at any rate he "knew"—because of his pals or the waiters.

It was no good my promising Leah a surprise or a present, or discretion on my part. I couldn't persuade her to come to my rooms. I could come and have an apéritif with her tomorrow, that was all. I needed her. She had pretty plump curves, and her hoarse voice enchanted me, ravished me. So much soft skin, smoothed with face creams, washed with unguents, so many jewels, precious meats, dyes, drugs, tenderness, at the service of those hairy legs, strong as connecting rods, now reposing preciously rolled in their coverings. It was a very illogical and yet natural game that I found myself thrust into, it was astonishing . . . and irritating, and in any case gave me, alone of all the fans, strength to sit out the night.

*

* *

Sunset. Grenadine. The hour was smooth as asphalt. Quiet descended despite the scorching of bitters. I waited for Leah in a brasserie near Porte-Maillot. She came down from Montmartre in a hired coupé, clothed in an otter coat, toward the watered apéritifs.

"It reminds me of my youth, when I first met Pettimatheu. I had a room by the month in the rue des Acacias."

My first request was for news of the race.

"A bit tired," she said. "Pain in the kidney, and colic. But the other leading team's got it too. The Aussie's off his feed. Touch of water on the knee. We'll leave it there. They've been crawling all the mornin'; want a tourist agency, eh what?"

"And Van den Hoven?"

"'E beefs on like a wild man, sure is. But he hasn't the head, not for the teamwork. It's Bibby and Pettimatheu who keep it together."

I perceived that seeing Leah again was not unalloyed pleasure. I liked her plebeian hands, her eyelids the color of a 50-franc note . . . her cold heart, magically softened by muscle; but I couldn't forget the race going on.

Drawn up at the curb, the consumers' autos exhausted the possibilities of form-combination. They were cannon, yachts, bathtubs, dirigibles. Others sketchily furnished with a champagne box. Their masters, these slicked-up young chaps, so handsome, watching the hours behind glass panes, Avenue Champs Élysées, in a tiled room where there is only one palm tree, a prayer rug, and a nickel-plated chassis. Like the women in the lower quarters of Amsterdam behind their show cases.

The waiters scurried from table to table holding black apéritifs between each pair of fingers. Mechanics in overalls, cyclists with tires wrapped round them, "pugs" coming from Cuny's, each man greeting his friends with the salutation of his guild. The bantams jabbed each other in the ribs; the three-quarters smacked each other's legs.

Leah was still pretty and refractory. Only my black-and-yellow tie, the team colors which I had bought specially, moved her. She wore a big white felt hat spiked with a vulture's feather and earrings, recalling Buffalo Bill and the ladies who hit the bull's-eye over their shoulder, sighting from a mirror. I told her that I wasn't a man like Pettimatheu, with a motto like "To the uttermost," and that I'd never been able to want anything for six nights running, that my doctor forbade me cold baths, that I had always behaved with horrible propriety, that my heart was a spare part, and that very thin curly-haired women have their charm.

She, on the contrary, seemed captivated to learn that I knew the Italian lakes and the author of "Tipperary," and that I possessed autographs of Marshal Joffre. I even boasted that there was the exact model of an Arab sheik's tent in my studio, and that I could play Tartini's "Devil's Trills" on the violin.

She looked at me:

"You aren't like anyone else."

"Thanks, Leah, women tell one these things; and yet it's with them, especially, that one is just like everyone else."

The automobile schools in the neighborhood threw off a fetid odor. One heard a hunt pass by beneath the fortifications, and that melancholy horn sounding under the Luna Park scenic railway—that dry dock for big steamers immobile in its bankrupt old shipyard.

*
* *

Arriving at the velodrome after a hollow day, I had to confess sourly that I came as much for the race as for Leah; nothing was changed on the poster board. But there was a sudden clearing of decks, the six racers revolved in a ribbon, mixing green, yellow, white, crimson, and orange. Their supple pedals continued to wear out the planks already worn smooth by revolving tires. They watched the starts when the bell rang.

Pettimatheu was in the saddle, he saw me and smiled recognition from his left eye. There was an attempt to break away from the 3,421st kilometer, the 131st hour. The balustrades groaned from the pressure of the cheap seat crowd, surprised during dinner with their mouths full.

The Negro with his nose on the handlebars shot out like an arrow, went half a lap ahead, and kept his lead. There was a tumult. Men who had been hurt from a fall, those who held their sides, those who had a bent wheel, were soon left behind, then doubled. Led by Pettimatheu the squad tore on behind the Negro, who began to weaken and look around; his mate was asleep and did not come to help him, the crowd yelled for him.

"Coco, dirty neck, get on to it."

A waiter dropped a glass of beer from the gallery. The place shook with the howling, rattles, whistles, until the Negro straightened up, put his hands on the center of the handlebars, continuing on his momentum to show that he'd had enough.

I went round to the racers' quarters.

Pettimatheu was beginning to dine, cleaned, shaved, pretty boy in a cashmere bathrobe, he held a cutlet in one hand and chewed into it.

Seated on the edge of the bed, Leah gazed at this mastication with damp and submissive eye. He offered me a cup of champagne and oeufs à la neige in a mixing box for liquid rubber.

I was proud to know this racer, "this tenor of the pedal," as the "p'og'am" called him. I began to take pride in his limber thighs, his impeccable knees. I showed my sympathy and encouraged him.

"I managed it," he said simply. "At that pace the nigger soon busted his guts. It's all in organization."

Pettimatheu surprised me chiefly by his calm, here he was dining peacefully like a citizen, only a few minutes after this chase, surrounded by diligent caretakers, by his loving female companion; sunk in cushions, with a screen of wisteria behind him, making a sort of privacy for him in the emptiness.

Leah held one of his fingers tenderly and said nothing. I felt equally fond of them both. I told them so.

We clicked glasses. Leah recited the toast:

> To our health which is dear to all of us
> and which we need so much
> because health brings money,
> and money buys sugar,
> and with sugar one can catch flies.

Pettimatheu explained his happiness:

"She's amusing, a good girl, too. She can cook and make poultices if necessary. And [has a] coachman by the month to blow his horn, he's a connoisseur in mushrooms. Well-educated, she is, full of conversation, makes one laugh in society. In private, a skin with veins like rivers in a geography book, hair right down to her heels (not merely three tufts like these modern women, who ain't got enough to tire a fine-tooth comb), some bosom, what, real packers' meat; diligent in bed, without putting half her back into it, brushes her teeth after eating, takes her asparagus with a specially made pair of tweezers, and never puts on a corset.

"You'll see when you know her better."

The orchestra played a scenic railway boston. Exquisite peaks, whence one was plunged into the languorous valleys of the refrains. Comedians in powdered chins came in from the theater. They wanted to dance, but the people called them fakers, woodenheads, sausage-eaters.

I left Pettimatheu in full swing, amusing his audience, pretending to be in bed with Leah in his "cabine."

127

I had to promise to come back tomorrow for the last heat and to stay the night.

*
* *

Sixth Night, 158th hour, 3,962 kilometer 570, same monotonous spectacle. The harassed squirrels slept in their whirligig, one hooked a wheel and fell, upsetting others. There were yells in English, Turkish oaths, the shrill clatter when some chap gave up; then the circle continued.

It was very late. The night sprints were over. The racers went round with their hands reversed to rest their wrists, wearing mufflers to keep off the night cold.

Pettimatheu reposed in his cage. Van den Hoven performed his obscure nocturnal duty leaving to his mate the brilliant work of the last hours now about to begin. I offered my services to Bibby, his face twisted spoonshape by fatigue. In our shirt-sleeves we dipped an inner tube in a bucket to find a puncture. Leah surprised me in this exercise. I was so preoccupied that I hardly answered. She grumbled. I shrugged my shoulders.

Many fans stayed the whole night. Children pink or pale slept on sporting papers. Platoons from the École Militaire, chauffeurs of the gentry, workmen from Moulineaux before going to the factories, shipping clerks going to their offices, provincial couples in mourning, yawned, kept themselves awake by playing euchre, and popped open their beer bottles.

"Eugene," said someone, "hand me the odorigène."

We rolled up in blankets, put sacks under our heads, and side by side awaited the dawn. Leah took my hand.

"What little bones! I feel that I'm goin' to take a fancy to you," she said, as they do in untrue popular ballads. Her voice was sweet and soapy. "You're just the opposite of a champion racer. You're more like a priest or a comic singer. You don't hardly talk, but you're lively. I always thought about liking someone that hadn't much health. A young artist or something, with an open collar, and his veins paley blue, and a nice little pointed beard—you can have me."

"Nothing would have given me greater pleasure, even yester-

128

day," I replied, caressing her. "And possibly tomorrow. But today my whole heart is here; I am the prey of a single thought: I want Pettimatheu to win. I do not belong to myself; neither do you. We have become part of the velodrome, an instant of the race, a waiting for the victory. A few hours more. Then think of the snapshots. The crowd, the special editions, the banquet with flags and deputies. We shall have contributed our little part in gaining all this for our conqueror."

"Dearie," said Leah, crossly, "you have a beautiful soul. It's lovely that. It's refined. I like you still better for it."

Disappointment twisted her lips.

She said nothing more. She closed her eyes. Then I heard her—but as if in a dream:

"I don't know how Pettimatheu will take it."

To our right above the Éternol Varnish ad, a desolate light appeared above the glass roof and was greeted by the machine piano. And I sang:

> The breechless cocks are singing each to each
> In the dirty bedclothes of the dawn
> Pink denials, flowers in garbage cans;
> My love has singularly diminished while you slept.

Hungarian Night

—

ود§ "Give me the long one, that one, with the big hips," said Jean with boozy insistence.

The other was hung with thin muscles, projecting veins, bracelet ligatures, phantom bones, and had the face of an animal marked for sacrifice.

In preferring her I felt the easy superiority that one feels in a dream, and, as in a dream, was puerilely happy in being able to say:

"I like that cross between a unicorn and a red jackass."

A dahlia fell into my open mouth and went halfway down my throat. Battle of flowers. A garden moved by in the air.

Nourished by Schubert's *Militär Marsch* the two Jewish girls danced on the platform, nervous, pathetic, unentangled by our melted glances, by the allegories of the smoke, by the glitter of glasses from which men with blue-shaved heads were slopping it down.

When the Tziganes had succumbed, the sisters Hajyz Nanas came down to speak to us, Jean's preference carrying her hair in her hand and offering for our amusement the domed skull of a Tangier merchant.

"It's a man, you're had."

"I'm had."

Despite its pretentious entrance, two palm trees, the admission price, two hundred kronen, the porter like a noble father from some An der Wien Theater play (in reality none other than General Rubinät of Premysl), the Jardin de Paris was a hole. But the only one of any importance open in Vienna in July 19— on the days when there was nothing on at the Belvedere.

Irritated by the lights, the chandelier wallowed like a crystal porcupine in the midst of Venetian mirrors reflecting cerise damask hangings and rococo boxes copied from Schönbrunn. Irreconcilable as a jazz band and a symphony orchestra, the women in long skirts kept down the women in short skirts. The former had in their favor a certain wheedling of the thighs, a way of saying "Mon cher"; pendants which opened, revealing the donor, a grand duke now hung, preserved there still in this ice of brilliants, souvenirs of Nice, memories of the Archduke Othon's luncheons at Negresco's, of the queen of Naple's parties, adieux of worn aigrettes, birds of a lost paradise; the supplications of their noble great hats from Lewis; and finally such a bitterness in their soft cheeks that the Greek parvenu Pisistrates, addressed as Pipi, finally abandoned himself.

The young could only score by their footwork, their nervous excess and compliances which won them the title of "modernists" from their female elders. When she had greeted me I offered my danseuse a glass of ersatz Tokay which was titubating in a Moselle bottle on our little gilt table.

"Where do you come from?"

She replied by her name:

"Zaël."

She was from Pest. Between us we had only a few words of German.

"And you?"

"From Paris."

"*Schlecht* Paris," she said, sticking her tongue out. Italian lieutenants blocked the entrance door, carnations in their cartridge belts; Rumanian commandants come to carry off cattle, chose sheep-headed women. The Reparations Commission partook moderately of the local champagne. Under the famished eyes of the waiters the plutocrats at No. 1 table stuffed foie gras into their all-concealing cheeks.

"My friend thought your dancing partner was your sister."

"He ain't in the family. He's from Gratz, his name is Samuel Ehrenfeld. Shall I make him come over here? Why you smile, little uncle?"

"It's funny, in French, to have a name like Samuel Field-of-Honor."

For two hundred and eighty kronen we procured dried herb cigars and saucers of currants. Zaël stuck a straw into them.

"What you say?"

"That you have a pretty little phiz," I answered, laying my finger on my cheek as they do in the pantomime.

Zaël perched on her chair with difficulty, and without equilibrium; this body of an Israelitish sylph, breastless, with delicate skin, a rounded back, the hands nervous, practical, too mature for their seventeen years.

"She's like the lot that chase down the rue de Rome when there's a test at the Conservatoire," said Jean. Then he continued the interview:

"What you think of Béla Kun?"

"Béla Kun," she delivered a eulogy in Yiddish, "he's in Vienna. But he's been King of Hungary, my little Uncle. He's very rich. Soon he will be king also in Vienna. Ehrenfeld says that he is much loved in Moscow and that he will also go into Italy. Then they will hang all the Hungarians who throw Jews down the wells."

When at 11:30 the street sucked in the audience from the Jardin de Paris, Zaël suggested the Moulin Rouge, with [a] private entrance on St. Petersplatz. This proved to be a Secession mausoleum in black marble, with festoons of stylized gold and a cross-beamed ceiling of beaten silver plaques studded with turquoise. The keeper, an ex-captain of the Guards with the face of a long jump champion, seated us at the edge of a dark carpet with wreaths of flowers woven into it. We swallowed an indigo liqueur. Zaël made friends with some Near Eastern rastas in pale gray shortcoats, soft collars, white socks, and pumps. In a remade coat, his candied face surrounded by filagree silver whiskers, an ex-government departmental head, for the moment without functions, served hard-boiled eggs from a little gilt basket slung from his neck on a pink ribbon.

Jean pretended to blow his nose. Zaël leapt on him with a small cry, seizing the cashmere handkerchief. Silk sent her crazy.

"Little uncle, please, give it to me for a souvenir."

"A parting gift, yes. We're going to Budapest tomorrow, by the Danube, because of the railway strike."

"Take me with you," this impetuously, "I want to see my grandfather again. He's the keeper of the synagogue."

"You haven't a passport."

"I know a Russian that makes 'em, down by the Südbahnhof, his name's Apotheoz."

Her manner is irresistible, except when she bites my arm to the bone, from excitement. I protest:

"The Eternal has said 'Thou shalt not eat of impurity.' "

She listens, her body immobile up to the eyes, but in them, under the bulging pupils, lie all the promises. Jean, melted, confesses in his turn the witchcraft. We go to a private room where a constipated lamp sputters amid satanic curtains.

"Drei cocktails." Cockroaches, already Oriental, scuttle over the gold-lacquered tables.

Zaël allows herself to be kissed without interrupting her argument.

"I hardly ever go to the synagogue except for the Great Atonement, when you empty your pockets, you know, and throw the things into the water. I've forgotten the Hebrew they taught me for initiation.

"Take me with you, grandfather is so old, so ill. I haven't seen him for a year and a half. If you don't I won't ever see him again. I am his star. It is written: 'Misfortune will come upon him who watcheth not over his ancestors and whose feet stay not in his house.' The old man never goes out, for fear of being assassinated. Say, I was born at a ball. They baptized me there in champagne. A year ago one of my brothers was assassinated at Szeged, they killed him with bludgeons. The other one, Samarie's in New York. We're all suspected by the officers. I'll go with you all the same, my little uncles, cause you're foreigners with white passports, and nobody'll dare say anything to me."

The little uncles sought their niece's bosom.

We went down a river ruffled by the north wind, between grain elevators set up like cement trumpets, tied together by little wheeled cars. For a moment longer, domes gone green, enslaved

133

palaces with broken windows, reviewed by bronze equestrian statues; Vienna, between her gasworks, amid her silent horde of the unemployed, bowed like a dowager in misfortune. One passed lighters loaded with war rubbish, filled almost to sinking with unbelievable bits of iron, barbed wire, wheels, rust, a whole country still giving up, in fragments. Then the Danube broadened out, looking like all the Nigers, mirroring only the sky, putting willows between herself and the plain, bracing herself against wheatless mills, hurrying from under the bridges . . .

Zaël was stretched out between Jean and myself in a steamer chair. She had put on her silk dress for the trip, a white satin ribbon round her forehead, her naked legs ending in velvet slippers. The trail of smoke rolled above our head over an awning that clacked in the wind.

"I am happy to be with my little uncles."

Then the Hungarian plain, the rustling of ripe wheat cut by acacia-bordered farms, freighted with hayricks, cosmetic'd with manure, all this gave way to mountains. The river narrowed again. Pine woods unrolled, keeping their alignment in spite of the slopes, cupboards, dark from their rim, in them villages each set round its bulbous belltower. As one got nearer to Pest, naked men and women were bathing and shouting along the banks. Boats freighted with the wail of accordions bobbed on our steamer's wake. Apricot vendors, in embroidered tunics, came aboard. After the Czechoslovak frontier, noncommissioned Magyar officers in threadbare dolmans, with mustaches twisted above dull turquoise teeth, came and inspected us.

The sun finally went down, like the tail of a cloudy peacock. Pest presented itself by factory chimneys and the odors of breweries and of tanbark; a twist of the river showed Buda: the big Regency houses, gardens and terraces, the jejune royal palace, stagy and savage. The big hotels, with all their windows lit up, lay at anchor along the promenades, hooked to the sky by the raspberry-colored light of their roof gardens.

At the Danubia Jean and I had the same room, Zaël's opened into it. The walls were still pitted by machine-gun bullets, plaster shaken off by enfilade from the monitors. One forgot the blanketing heat in the cheek-piercing sting of paprika'd food, assuageable only in weak Pressburg wine that tasted of silex. We slept through the day, with shutters closed to an ocher Danube in full irridescence; the river coated the bastions of the Burg with lime, beneath the scorched gardens in which nothing but colored glass balls still managed to flower.

Then, in the evening, the town woke. Tziganes commenced their commentary in the restaurations, dolorous altos, lethargic boxes of cellos, dull cymbalums like harps scourged with felt rods. Women dressed in muslins and light pongees, their hands and faces sun-beaten, watched the interallied auto patrol, not moving at the squawk of its motorhorns; the chauffeurs leaned out to pinch them.

After the second day we were shadowed, tough mugs slouched about us. Despite our curses the porter failed to return Zaël her passport, pretending that the police hadn't yet sent it back. We were advised not to leave the hotel in the evening. Encouraged by the impotence of the authorities, gangs of unpaid officers roamed the streets, holding up pedestrians and sandbagging Jews and the foreigners.

We went with Zaël to the synagogue. The quarter viewed our visit with uneasiness. When we stopped for too long we caught sight of terrified eyes behind counters. They were closing the shops. Galician Jews, in sheepskin coats, with greasy tufts of side whiskers in front of their ears, their shoulders powdered with dandruff, were selling pamphlets on Zionism, wax synagogue tapers, and coats of dyed sheepskin. The courtyards communicated with each other like rabbit warrens, a balcony on each floor, in each court a tree, an unhitched horse, unfed children.

"The synagogue," squealed Zaël, sniffing the Jewish smells of the stairs with open nostrils. "Wait a minute."

She came down again, without having effected an entrance. The old man was barricaded inside and didn't dare open the door. Soldiers in shabby uniforms were on the landing at service hours and wouldn't let people in. They had chased her away. "Their feet run to evil," she said, "and they have haste to shed blood."

On our way back to the hotel, we noticed that we were followed.

We went to bed about midnight. Zaël came to drink and smoke in our room, then undressed in her own, asking us to leave the door open between them. She behaved as usual. She bagged still another handkerchief and danced a mazurka in her chemise.

In the middle of the night, Jean woke me:

"I don't hear anything, but I think something has happened while we were asleep."

We switched on the electric light. It was three o'clock. I leapt out of bed and looked into the next room. Zaël was no longer there. The door into the hall was open, the bedclothes thrown back, clothes on the floor. There was a man's footprint on the pillow. A smell of pharmacy in the air.

"Chloroform," said Jean.

We rang. No one answered. Finally the night porter came up; a slate-gray Neapolitan, the complexion of watchers. He had heard nothing, seen nothing. No one had left the hotel.

"But a person can't disappear like this from a hotel in these days," I said. "We'll go to the police."

The Neapolitan smiled.

I got excited:

"We must have the place searched from cellar to attic!"

"There is no attic, Monsieur. As for the cellar . . . certainly, the Danubia is a palace, but I don't know anyone who would risk himself down there in these days. The cellars are quite extensive. They communicate with the Danube . . . Believe me, Monsieur, I don't want to alarm you but you would do better to have a look round by the dam at St. Margaret's Island, in say another few hours."

Borealis

⌇ The Gothic porch was lit by a lamp, 200 candlepower. I stopped on the opposite sidewalk. Men entered, alone; others, with women. I hesitated, my heart beating fast, devoid of heroism, until the arrivals ceased. Ungracious stairs led to a door before which were traces of sawdust. The anteroom smelt of gas and dried sweat. A girl with plaits read my temporary membership card—a small parchment hexagon—and I penetrated to the men's dressing room. Shirts hung there, emptied of bodies; suspenders reposed there; boots lifted their rubber heels, for the Norse foot had not escaped the wave of American exports which burst over Eastern Europe the day after the armistice, in guise of calculating machines, fly-killers, and dental floss. A nickel shoehorn shone from the middle of the floor.

Should I undress here? The notices on the wall doubtless instructed one, but how was one to understand letters that looked like toads and insects, covered over with curlicues, with their innumerable accentuation of pimples and air bubbles? I removed my shoes and half opened the door. The costume was of mosque rather than of club, for I caught sight of two members in what I may call the requirements. One faced me, leaning sideways on a balustrade. A wisp of hair, wound about his head like a fungus, gave the first slender promise of the white beard which flowed downward over his chest, there mingling with a thick tufty growth such as one sees in secondhand shops bulging out of old sofas. Thence the body hair divided itself into two regular strips, edging, each, one side of the stomach. It foamed for an instant, then subsided in ivylike fantasy about the legs and terminated its course with the feet. His interlocutor faced him, thus having his back to me. He had black unbendable hair. The branches of gold spectacles glittered behind his ears. He also was naked and moved the big toe of his right foot in rhythm.

I closed the door and sat down. I should have no difficulty in stripping or in moving naked; since childhood I have known fencing schools, sporting clubs, swimming pools, and Turkish baths. Neither did I fail to remember that I was here of my own free will, having asked for admission as a foreign member to the Diana Bund, or Society of Diana.

Without going back to the fifteenth century, when, after the Hussite schism, people in Bohemia founded sects favoring Adamic nudity as a means of salvation (which proved in the end only a means of getting massacred), I had heard often of Germanic groups whose members assemble in order to live without clothing. The reading of a Teutonic review consecrated to the propagation of nudity and to questions of aesthetics and hygiene, i.e., eugenics, had put me on the track and indicated to me the existence of Nordic branches of this new mutuality: Nacktkultur. An ad in the Swedish review *Beauty* finished the matter:

"Persons of both sexes, of Aryan race, desiring to join a serious society whose aims are those of the review *Beauty,* are invited to write to P.O. Box 78, at . . . . Branches in Nordic countries."

Being later in . . . ., I wrote to the indicated address, enclosing a stamp for reply and received a letter-card whereon a Dr. Vulpius requested me to explain more clearly my reasons for wishing to join the Society and to state my age, profession, etc. I sent the doctor a declaration of principles in harmony with the review, citing the great ancient civilizations, the festivals of Sparta, the laws of Lycurgus, the Germans of Tacitus' time. I animadverted also, from a medical point of view, on the benefits derivable from the chemical effects of sun on the cuticle.

They gave me a rendezvous, for two days later, at the Café Odin, first floor, Prince Alexander Room, where there was to be an evening of lectures with lantern slides and at which I would meet the executive committee.

It was seven in the evening, after dinner. The café opened on the wood port. Norwegian sailing ships with icy spars, a lone reminder of snow recently melted, raised their cross-trees level with the double windows from which the paper glued there to keep out the cold had not yet been torn away. A night breeze distorted the waves between us and some islands which sloped gently into the water, at an angle taken also by the launching ways freighted with freshly caulked keels flaming with red lead and the sunset.

The president (Dr. Vulpius, as I learned) was blind and supported a pair of black spectacles upon a landscape of facial blotches. He discoursed solemnly from the center of the platform, flanked by the vice-president and the treasurer. The latter was a tortoise-headed blonde, doubtless an officer's widow, wearing glasses and terminating in a hat bordered with jonquils. Her eye cast forth its scrutative beam to-me-ward, and it sank in like a grappling iron. Like a boarding party, her thought rose to encounter my thought, and I felt that my admission depended, in ultimate, on this vigilant guardian of the nunnery's turning-box.

I used English for my explanation. My remarks were translated to a young girl concealed behind the paper of her typewriter. This secretary then expressed herself in the dialect of the locality. My French citizenship aroused more interest than sympathy and stirred them to no trust.

"Is it clearly understood that no curiosity of an immoral nature has moved you to ask for admission to this Society?"

"We admit only persons of proved respectability, who are not given to drink or to Theosophy, who do not read immoral books, and who have regular incomes."

The assessor on the right, a red-bearded man of forty, wearing a frock coat, with politeness pursued the examination.

"Do you associate with Russians? Or Jews?"

After I had shown my passport and made a deposit, the jury deliberated in an undertone. Then the typewriter clicked.

"You will be admitted for two months, after you have passed the medical examination. You will be given a visitor's membership. Will you please wait in the anteroom?"

I rose as the door opened. The typist entered, offering me an envelope and a smile, from which I gathered that the sentence was favorable. All the bashfulness was on my side. The prestige of a serious manner, of these silences, of these frank and natural gestures, is sudden. My sympathy moved toward her instantly. She had blue eyes bordered with black lashes falling evenly as a fringe, a courteous mouth, and short hair tinseled with pale refractions.

I was on the point of getting excited, of bursting into conversation, but she suddenly clicked her heels together and made me an adorable, extremely rapid low bow; a sort of shiver from calves to pate. Her hair flopped forward, shaking over her forehead, and she left the room without speaking.

The next day I passed the medical examination in a suburban hospital, full of lice left by Kronstadt refugees. I was examined by a doctor and consultants. The process was speedy, but rigorous. All contagious diseases, including bad breath and intestinal worms, ended one's chances, likewise any skin trouble or any physical deformity likely to damage the aesthetic pleasure of one's fellow members.

I was received, permitted to pay my subscription and to acquaint myself with the bylaws. My anxiety increased on reading and inwardly marking that: "The least infraction of the Society's ideal, or any indecency likely to shock the delicacy of the members, leads to instant expulsion."

Thus and now with no other garment than turquoise ring, I might, with head held high, enter the hall of games where twice weekly the members of the Diana Bund strip themselves and pass an evening in the costume of Paradise. I was about to be one of them. The thing was sanctioned by the police and considered perfectly natural, without seeming, to me, wholly so. Admitted that my apprehension diminished on remembering earlier Nordic experiences, mixed sunbaths on the German strands of the Baltic, Swedish hydrotherapies wherein one is delivered to gentle feminine hands that seem to have been worn down by soap, Russian bathing beaches where I had seen men and their companions scorched and naked, with arms around each other's waists in island waters blue as your fountain pen's ink. The idea of finding myself among wives and young ladies was, for all that, disturbing. I half opened the door again. On the platform with its adornment of flags, golden palms, snakes pickled in oil, a third conversationalist had joined the two others. He wore, slung around his neck, a black shagreen case revealing the form of a reservoir pen, but there could be no question of underdrawers or of a towel for even a neophyte; time was moving. I was obviously, the last to unclothe. I entered the hall with measured tread, resolute, with a dry throat and hands clenched.

I noticed at once a "restauration" where naked families in rattan armchairs partook of radishes and café au lait. It was as in the Turkish bath, after the hot room. A lady who held her knitting propped against her abdomen appeared to me as an evil dream. I heard calls, cries; the floor shook with stamping. Balls rolled with the noise of thunder, smashing the ninepins. I found myself in the center of a glass-covered hall, walled with pine planks, smeared with yacht varnish, like everything else in that country. Forty people of both sexes were taking exercise. A group of men did the high jump over a rope that was moved up two centimeters at a time. A naked gentleman looking like the king of Sweden wrecked in revolution phlegmatically adjusted it after each turn. I concentrated my attention upon them forcibly, thus keeping it off the opposite sex. The gymnastic appliances were at the other end of the room. In the sawdust, isolated amateurs raised and lowered themselves or limbered their dorsal muscles with Indian clubs. Youthful athletes cast javelins against mattresses. In the pauses, they imbibed ice water, rinsed their mouths therewith, and spat it far from them on the floor. Elderly ladies maneuvered hexagonal promenades on one foot, or executed triangular hop-skips as if they were victims of some system of penitence.

The shock of trapeze rings clacking together drew my attention. I lifted my eyes, which until then had been lowered in nunlike abasement, and saw suspended above me a curious ball of limbs, knotted together, with round knees and sharp elbows projecting. The object slowly revolved over itself, a pink rump rose from the projections of vertebrae, impelled by the wrist muscles, a straining of the neck forced a head through ash-blonde forelocks which were caught back by a large black silk ribbon bow. It smiled, and I recognized Dr. Vulpius' typist, precisely—the one from whom I had received my certificate. She paused, froglike, in her rings, indolent, sinuous, at her ease, the smile dropping upon me from her Nordic and goblin, fresh, irregular face. I felt needle points under my scalp. Again the blonde head plunged earthward, the arms opened at right angles; stretched out and above this axis, the body sought a deliberate readjustment; the legs came together and reached the floor in a quarter circle.

I had then before me the body of an adolescent athlete which left no room for improvement. I dared not take my eyes from the face. The damsel smiled and saluted me. I felt her breath on my arms. I cut short the pantomime, brusquely turned my back on her, rushed to the high jump, joined the persevering squad; I leapt to the springboard like a dervish—my foot caught in the rope, I went flat, smashed my nose, arose with satisfaction and with bleeding hands. I felt the need of continuing, of not letting my eyes return toward the female. What eyes! I fell upon the trapeze. I straddled the parallel bars. What lips, what lip corners! And so clement! I lifted the forty-pound dumbbells. What a breast without blemish! I embarked on a series of jumps, wherein my Aryan energy won the esteem of all present. Short-winded, out of training, sweating, I had to stop before long. And she, she was before me! Eve with bobbed hair, without embarrassment, shameless before the fall, stretching out arms not humped into biceps and triceps but covered with the long flowing muscles, such as one sees in swimmers. I was breathless.

"My name is Aïno," she said, using German for this explanation. "My parents ask if you will take a glass of tea with us."

I delivered myself to her guidance. A fat man whose fleece obscured any precise silhouette, her father, politely invited me to be seated. Director of the Baltika Hereditas Insurance Co. The young brother was squeezing spring dumbbells to develop his hand muscles. The mother held her two plate-sized breasts firmly between her two elbows. She was reading Fichte and gave me a hyacinth to smell. Her arms were still young, only the face and belly were wrinkled. I reached for my trouser pockets and found none in my thighs. Sneezed.

She said: "You'll soon get used to doing without your clothes. We live this way at home. In summer we go naked to pick strawberries, and in winter we break a hole in the ice to go bathing. The antique Beauty is not extinct, as the Lutherans tell you. No, Monsieur. She is like the swallows who, as our peasants believe, pass the winter in the lake bottoms and who always return."

She spoke to her young son:

"If you bite your nails, you'll ruin your hands, and then you'll be thrown down the big well."

It was all going so nicely. I took tea with lemon, in the midst of these robust burghers in whom one could perceive respectable habits and a certain prosperity. Café au lait, cucumbers, and acacia fritters fit for the Scandinavian gods were offered on giant reed hurdles. The father took a fancy to me and showed me the ravine which a most unusual operation had left in his abdomen. His company would insure, upon request, against appendicitis, with underwriting by Lloyd's. He spoke of the nutritive power of vegetables. I looked, in secret, at Aïno. When I met her eyes, or when my pleasure became excessive, I turned my gaze against some counterfeit corpus, I lowered it against the deformed feet of my interlocutors, between which naked infants struggled, toppled over by monstrous heads, and wallowed like lion cubs. No longer fearful of being judged heretic, I resisted no inquiry, forbade myself no exploration. The worst, I thought, must be over.

Then someone ordered collective games. Cat and mouse produced no disorder. We formed a great circle. The cat tried to catch the mouse; we delayed the cat with a thousand obstructions. We laughed, puffed. There was an armistice. The game of fox and geese followed; a sort of human chain, a sportive snake dance in which each person grasped firmly the waist of the person antecedent. The fox tried to capture the gosling. The line undulated, gave way, and reformed in its attempt to save the prey from the hunter. Aïno was behind me. Her hands cut into my flanks like hot knives. She laughed and told me not to give way. I avoided her contact, thus anchoring myself more firmly to a young blonde female, ugly, solid as a bridge pile, who bent her legs to lower her center of gravity and offer less prise to the bumps. Conscientious and lymphatic, she pushed out an enormous rump which veritably creaked with the effort. My recoil from this pressed Aïno against me. The struggle for the moment was especially active. I felt her arms round my waist, all her body was crushed against mine with an unbearable leverage, her panting breast was pasted into my back. I closed my eyes, and a curious restlessness came upon me. It was shame unspeakable and uncomfortable, mixed with a sort of drowsiness. I wanted to stay there all my life. The chain almost broke at every new buffet. With a sudden movement, I let go my hold on the fat girl and broke loose also from Aïno. I leapt from the crowd, casting no glance behind me, ascended the stairs with impetuosity, and closed the door of the dressing room firmly.

In the street the cold came against my cheeks like the charge from a gun loaded with rock salt. I felt light as a pigeon and wholly soaked with electricity.

*
* *

I met Aïno two days later, in a bun shop.

"You don't recognize me?"

"Almost. If you are Aïno, you have beauty spots on your right breast and left shoulder. But who can tell in these clothes?"

"What do you wear that hair for? A man ought to shave his head every morning. You don't wear a slide chain round your neck with a private diary at the end of it? How far can you throw the hammer? Do you always walk round-shouldered?"

I urged her to dine with me or anyhow to make a date.

"I'll come for you tomorrow with the motorcycle. We'll go to G . . . for St. John's Eve. Bring a suitcase."

We crossed the town, nodding at every bump; the horn obtained us a passage, as it were, in thin slices. The bystanders offered little resistance. When the tramway blocked the pebbled street, we veered toward the sidewalk, grazing old impotent cabs painted in raw color, squashed down under their astrakhan-capped coachmen; from beneath the troika yokes, the little horses shook their forelocks and turned red eyes upon us. We went by curious buildings; the court house, the prefecture of police, Greek temples dating from the first Russian occupation; in the façades of German shipping offices stood bearded caryatids—the directors, apparently—naked from the waist up. Under a punishing wind they sold all sorts of things made of birchwood, valises, bicycles, beds; in the shops, the imports, canned tongue, and safety razors with the portrait of General Krabb tied to each by yellow ribbons. Our reflection covered most of the windows. It slid over them, confusing the products inside or enveloping them in its transparency. Me in the red-varnished coffin, with disheveled projecting hair, streaming eyes; the wheel made oval by the pace showed under my cramped legs, and above my flat image rose Aïno's: green sweater, legs booted up to the hips in oiled leather, her short hair torn by the wind, softening with its blonde luster, a pleasant dementia; the dark malevolent mask of barred spectacles muzzling the upper part of her face and fitting down to the line of her mouth, heavy, young, reassuring. Aïno drove the cycle with concentration, insensitive to the smell of rank oil or the banging of defective explosions, shutting off the spark and my breath, simultaneously, at the crossroads, more often jamming on the brake, glancing over her thigh at the exhaust or smiling at me under her elbow.

There were no suburbs. The country began, straight away, at the ground floor of a five-story house. A few clouds dropped their carpet of shadows on the roadway. The sky above the lakes was so clear that the sea gulls showed crow-black against it. Still a few places belonging to the owners of the paper factory; wireless masts rose from their roofs. We crossed athletic grounds set in the clearings of pine woods; the athletes were there at practice. We scorched down a sort of torn ribbon that flattery might have labeled a road. I bent over, twisted my sides, lifted myself by my hands to lessen the jolting. Aïno grinned; the nearer I came to being thrown out, the better she liked it. She encouraged me with phrases lost on the wind. Later, nothing but silver birches, black rimmed, a vegetable funeral notice, interrupted by pools girded with rheumatic willows, twisted, arthritic; drowned tree trunks drifted toward the sawmills: a promise of so many pink-headed matches.

I had left the Champs-Élysées a month before, the trees were already giving shade; the Ambassadeurs was being repainted, banners flowered before the salon; the tire-polished asphalt flowed down to the Concorde, like deep water. And I regretted it all. Nothing but birches. I would have given my life for a chestnut tree. The cupolas were green in Dresden, the lilacs had flowered; in Sweden they were unscrewing the ice-breakers, they were putting the yachts in commission; here these trees had leaves in small format. Going north in this way was like running the spring film backward. Still the birches (this time the slim trunks cut into

145

wood piles), locomotives drawing them stacked on flat cars and ringing a bell as they pulled. Green and russet smoke belched from the bell-mouthed smokestacks, less pleasing to the eye than blue coal smoke, but bringing back to us, lapped on the wind, the sharp intoxicating perfume of vegetation. Wooden scaffolds for the ski matches stretched up uselessly, stripped by the thaw and showing the undersides of their framework.

I was happy. I took Aïno's hand and stroked her wrist very gently, this cutting off the spark and stopping the cycle abruptly. I clasped her in my arms. She stood up on the pedals, pushed the goggles back on her forehead, broke her comb, tried to tidy her hair with spread fingers.

"A French girl wouldn't do this, eh? I had a French friend once. Her head was so big she was always falling over herself. She couldn't hold anything in her hands; her gloves, her sachet, or her handbag, something was always falling off her, like a ripe fruit, when she moved."

"My friends," I replied with annoyance, "order their clothes by telephone, scrub floors, and never have bellyache. But none of them has your complete dearth of eloquence, or such sunburn, or a body that will slide through trapeze rings like cashmere."

And to be even with her:

"I thought your compatriots ate soap and worshiped crow-headed idols."

This wooden house, painted the color of bull's blood, with white framed windows, perched on chunks of granite, is the G . . . They had scratched the Russian lettering off the door.

Our two rooms were so near together, so identical with their yellow curtains, their furniture of silky birch, their towering white porcelain stoves, their double windows with hyacinths growing between them, that I would soon be unable to distinguish one from the other. It was so clean, I didn't know where to put my cigarette ash.

"We'll have a cold supper and then go to bed."

"So soon?" I said. "Hadn't we better wait until dinner time?"

She smiled. I looked at my watch and found that it was eleven in the evening.

The table swarmed like a fishnet with salmon, speckled trout, herring, anchovies in packets of six, their tails tied together; the drink being milk and beer of an unfermented variety. I drew a flask of Norwegian brandy out of my sponge bag. Aïno clapped her hands, uncorked the bottle with a hair pin, sneezed with pleasure. She filled two glasses level, offered me one, took the other, stood at attention, clicked her heels and her tongue, and emptied her glass instanter, bowed and turned the bottom of it toward me with some unintelligible salutation. She had removed her hip boots and put on a house frock covered with peasant embroidery; a necklace of vegetable ivory wandered over her like a sort of vague second dentition. We ate in silence like a couple of Britishers. Aïno's cheeks shone, without rouge powder, like all other Scandinavian faces in which the quick blood spreads its cosmetic, enforced by the open air or by the least trifling attention. Two bottles yielded their eloquence. Our heads were buzzing.

The laws demand temperance. But they like a foreigner to arrive at table with bottles of Benedictine. Drunk by glassfuls, it adds savor to the fish diet. I have heard that good fortune has thus been found for small outlay, though the man who said it added that it was, for all that, expensive. My suitcase held a small cellar. I made several cocktails, complicated and despotic: a "corpse-waker" I had learned from the barman in the Grand Hotel, Stockholm, an "interior caress" picked up in Denmark. Aïno imbibed them with simplicity, contentment and a calm which prevented me from asking her to take her chemise off. She wandered around the table, composing piscine sonatas, her feet dragging from wearing snowshoes all winter. When she came near me, I insisted upon the strength of my desire to plant a kiss on her nostrils. She made no objection. Her flesh gave off the odors of tar and encaustic. I took her head in my hands and enumerated her features. She was the Mongolian type, flat nosed with the sunken eyes which make her compatriots look like vermillioned Chinese.

I emitted the stupid Occidental interrogatory: "And your family?"

"It's St. John's Eve. They'll think I'm sleeping at G . . ."

I was moved by the grace of this rectitude, by these savage confessions, by this whole system that we have so long dreamed of substituting for our pretexts, our indirectness and the threadbareness of our fables.

Like the night, hypocrisy was here reduced to nothing: baths of frankness, baths of the midnight sun.

"Aïno, you are not in a sweat, you do not indulge in the cruel pleasure of doubting me, you demand nothing of the stars; you are without guile, without chignon; in Paris my friends would take you for a glorified laundress. You are a young girl, and yet you do not look like a decoy; others call themselves musicians until eleven p.m. You stand solid on your legs, you don't sprain your ankles, you don't wear out the carpet in front of your looking glass."

"I like Frenchmen, because they never give a girl five minutes' peace."

"Yes, we manage to have a good time in Paris—on condition that we take them out in the afternoon, entertain them in the evening, caress them at night, let them alone in the morning. And then, none of our blondes is really blonde, blonde like this."

"Blasphemy!"

"I adore sunburn, black-and-blue marks on the skin, scratches on the knees, the marks of kisses, sunstrokes, skin that stays white under the hair, everything that you are, your modesty, your consistency, your fingers without rings. I have passed the age when a man thinks he's the only one a woman has ever fallen in love with."

I held her large red hand, content with having already seen Aïno naked, sure there was no mistake possible, no possible side-slip. I knew what was before me. None of the calamities hidden beneath faked pretences, such as I had suffered aforetime, the rodomontade of dresses, the ingenuity of veils in fragile penumbras, the chemise that they will keep on till the last, like a conjurer's handkerchief, to facilitate their devices.

Aïno had started to give me a full list of all the fauna of the country, of all the animals who live on islands and fish who live in pools so exactly suited to them in each case that one would think the former had been made out of the earth of which the latter had been relieved. Penguins set on cliffs of guano, like jars in a pharmacy, beavers with pompadours, owls, grand dukes in white cotton wool, seals oiled up like cannon, brown bears who scratch the northernmost trees of the planet, horned reindeer among the granites, all the glacial splendor, the ceremonies of the thaw, the magic of their summer.

"Got any whiskey?" said Aïno. "I love whiskey. When I can't get it, I drink toothwash. Makes me feel that I am sa-a-a-iling."

I noticed for the first time that she was drunk. But she neither laughed loudly, broke her glass with her teeth, or took off her shoes under the table; she went on munching insipid watery pickles, drying her mouth on a paper napkin, kissing me full on the lips, and calling me "Püppchen." There it was: the desired moment—when the Poles tell you about the jewels they have stolen, when the Germans copy out verses, when the Americans tell you to put out the Negroes, when the Negresses yield to engineers, when the Spaniards object to being kissed because "the lips were made to receive the Holy Communion"; when the English ask for their money.

I wanted to take her in my arms. She made an effort to rise, went limp, said: "But-t-i-am-not . . ." fell on the floor, with arms stretched.

I laid her on the bed. She breathed heavily. Her frock opened like bark. I saw once more the breasts firmly attached to the shoulders by pectoral muscles made strong with rowing. I put a cold water compress on her forehead. Her legs were open and full of shadow.

She said: "No." She half opened her eyelids, glued together like those of a new born kitten, sat up, and wanted to vomit.

Spike-shod constellations shone already upon us. The accordion lost its breath now and then, twisted, like a cut worm. Aïno and I stood at the bow of the ferryboat. Similar couples laughed, the gulls likewise. We were now halfway to the islands whence stray phrases, fragments of noise already reached us. The tips of the pine trees were turning purple.

Aïno had slept till midday, had got up once to drink two quarts of water. She searched my pockets and found a flask of Josephine brandy. I threatened to throw it overboard. She looked up at me with the transparent eye of Virginia and butted me like a goat.

I was still annoyed that she had escaped, thanks to this lethargy.

Her silence was like the mute reproach of indigènes: "Wicked white man, you brought the firewater." I thought I had better explain:

"My country is the land of the wine, of temperance, of sociabil . . ."

"Don't quarrel, one mustn't quarrel on St. John's Night."

The caged sun went down between tree trunks, like a red slice of beetroot. The ferryboat came into dock. Two anchors fell from its nostrils. It was midnight, the hour of strangeness, orange hued, striped russet with zebra stripes. Columns of steam rose from the lakes. We took a path on which fishbones, bits of paper, lace edgings of underwear, became fewer. A glare of bonfires lit on giant granites spread over the island. Other flames drifted on the water.

"Stop," said Aïno near the fountain which strengthens the sight. "These fires are in imitation of the sun and are meant to incite his return; these stones are sexual symbols."

"I would rather," I answered tartly, "you went on calling me Püppchen."

On the ground, in the shadow, couples were conciliating each other, silent, insensible to our presence, shut from the world by pleasure as if by a solid wall. We stepped over them. Elsewhere the sports were more noisy, there were songs, pistol shots. Under the sorb trees, young girls divided grass blades between them for divination. The smell of hot pine needles and roasting brioche came to us. People were jumping into the fires with legs and arms spread, making wishes in the midst of the flames. Fabulous shadows stalked over the earth or struggled between the blazes.

I urged Aïno to tell me her life story. She was studious but fanciful, "chimérique." Last year she had been secretary to the Boundary Commission and had, on that occasion, treated with the Bolsheviks. She had had a uniform with gold braid made for her in Stockholm and a two-pointed hat with vulture feathers, which she wore on the day of the signing. Feeling, suddenly, that her middle was more comfortable, she noticed that I had unhooked her dress during the narration.

I mumbled in circumlocution.

"I never undress except with the family," said Aïno.

Then we sat in the middle of a clearing. Cows emitted the odor of sour milk, and one smelt it thus close to the earth. We heard the tender groans by which the women were inciting their large-handed, lethargic companions. Someone fell with a raucous cry into an abyss, invisible; bones crackled like dead wood breaking.

"What are you thinking?" said Aïno.

"The simple grandeur of these Saturnalia moves my French soul," I responded, "which is salacious, deceptive, indiscreet. I have known the parks in New York—in August they are open all night to the public. In the warm dampness the greenswards become provisory cemeteries where workmen lie in their shirts with the Irish girls. Now and again a Neapolitan mechanic lifts up his tenor voice; the Slavs sing sometimes in chorus. In Hyde Park in winter, couples sit with mouths joined, amid the sheep, with fog up to their shoulders, enjoying themselves under the noise of the Salvation Army. In Madrid, in Plaza de Recoletos, behind the autos from the Ritz, muleteers in black velvet refresh themselves in the calico petticoats of two-penny whores. In Tahiti, damp herds of women swim out to the boats and board them. In Paris, in the ditches of the fortifications, kinky-haired youths . . ."

Aïno threw her arms round my neck.

"You are an international pig," said Aïno.

I took her in my arms. She remained there for the rest of the night; that is to say for something under ten minutes, for the sun, after a rapid ablution, was already upon us.